ABOUT THE AUTHOR

Christopher Pike was born in New York, but grew up in Los Angeles, where he still lives. Before becoming a writer, he worked in a factory, painted houses and programmed computers. His hobbies include astronomy, meditating, running and making sure his books are prominently displayed in his local bookshop. As well as being a bestselling children's writer, he is also the author of three novels for adults.

More books by Christopher Pike,
The Master of Fear

Last Act
Spellbound
Gimme A Kiss
Remember Me
Remember Me 2, The Return
Remember Me 3, The Last Story
Scavenger Hunt
Fall Into Darkness
See You Later
Witch
Master of Murder
Monster
Road To Nowhere
The Eternal Enemy
Die Softly
Bury Me Deep
Whisper Of Death
Chain Letter
Chain Letter 2, The Ancient Evil
The Immortal
The Wicked Heart
The Midnight Club
The Final Friends Trilogy
The Lost Mind
The Visitor
The Last Vampire
The Last Vampire 2, Black Blood
The Last Vampire 3, Red Dice
The Last Vampire 4, Phantom
The Last Vampire 5, Evil Thirst
The Last Vampire 6, Creatures of Forever

PIKE

THE LAST
VAMPIRE 2

Black Blood

*Hodder
Children's
Books*

a division of Hodder Headline plc

Copyright © 1994 by Christopher Pike

First published in the USA in 1994 as an Archway Paperback by
Pocket Books, a division of Simon & Schuster Inc.

First published in Great Britain in 1995
by Hodder Children's Books

The right of Christopher Pike to be identified as the Author of
the Work has been asserted by him in accordance with the
Copyright, Designs and Patents Act 1988.

10 9 8 7 6 5 4

All rights reserved. No part of this publication may be
reproduced, stored in a retrieval system, or transmitted,
in any form or by any means without the prior written
permission of the publisher, nor be otherwise circulated
in any form of binding or cover other than that in which
it is published and without a similar condition being
imposed on the subsequent purchaser.

All characters in this publication are fictitious
and any resemblance to real persons, living or dead,
is purely coincidental.

A Catalogue record for this book is available from
the British Library

ISBN 0 340 61170 7

Printed and bound in Great Britain by
Mackays of Chatham PLC, Chatham, Kent

Hodder Children's Books
A division of Hodder Headline plc
338 Euston Road
London NW1 3BH

For Teli

604408
MORAY COUNCIL
Department of Technical
& Leisure Services

JCY

504402

1 〜

I walk the dark and dangerous streets of L.A. gangland. A seemingly helpless young woman with silky
blond hair and magnetic blue eyes. Moving down
filth-strewn alleys and streets where power is mea-
sured in drops of blood spilled by bullets sprayed from
adolescent males who haven't learned to drive yet. I
am near the housing projects, those archaic hotels of
hostility where the checkout fee is always higher than
the price of admission. Because of my supernormal
senses, I know I am surrounded by people who would
slit my throat as soon as ask the time of day or night.
But I am not helpless or afraid, especially in the dark
at night, for I am not human. I, Alisa Perne of the

twentieth century, Sita of the ancient past. I am five thousand years old, one of the last of two vampires.

But are there only two of us left? I ask myself.

Something is terribly wrong in gangland L.A., and it makes me wonder. In the last month the *Los Angeles Times* has reported a string of brutal murders that leads me to believe Ray and I are not the only ones with the special blood that makes us impervious to aging and most other human ailments. The victims of these murders have been ripped open, decapitated, and, in some cases, the articles say, drained of blood. It is this last fact that has brought me to Los Angeles. I myself like blood, but I am not eager to find more vampires. I know what our kind can do, and I know how fast we can multiply once the secret of procreation is known. Any vampire I may find this evening will not live to see the light of dawn, or perhaps I should say the setting of the moon. I am not crazy about the sun, although I can bear it if I must.

A full moon rides high above me as I step onto Exposition Avenue and head north, not far from where the last murder occurred—a sixteen-year-old girl found yesterday in the bushes with both her arms torn off. It is late, after midnight, and even though it is mid-December, the temperature is in the midsixties. Winter in Los Angeles is like a moon made of green cheese, a joke. I wear black leather pants, a short-sleeved black top that shows my sleek midsection. My black boots barely sound as I prowl the uneven sidewalks. I wear my hair pinned up beneath a black cap. I love the color black as much as the color red. I know I look gorgeous. Cool stainless steel touches my right calf where I have hidden a six-inch blade, but otherwise I am unarmed. There are many police cars out this fine winter night. One passes me on the left as I lower my head and try to look like I belong. Because I fear being stopped and searched, I do not carry a gun. But it is only for the lives of the police that I fear, and not for my own. A whole S.W.A.T. team couldn't stop me. Certainly, I decide, a young vampire will be no match for me. And he or she must be young to be killing so recklessly.

But who is this youngster? And who made him or her?

Disturbing questions.

Three young males wait for me a hundred yards down the street. I cross to the other side, but they move to intercept me. One is tall and slim, the other squat as an old stump. The third has the face of a dark angel brought up on the wrong side of the pearly gates. He is clearly the leader. He smiles as he sees me trying to get away from him and his buddies, flexing his powerful biceps as if they were laws unto themselves. I see he carries a gun under his dirty green coat. The others are unarmed. The three jog toward me as I pause to consider what to do. Of course, I could turn and flee. Even if they were in training for the Olympics, they couldn't catch me. But I don't like to run from a fight, and I am suddenly thirsty. The smile of the leader will fade, I know, as he feels the blood drain from his body into my mouth. I decide to wait for them. I don't have long to wait.

"Hey, babe," the leader says as they surround me in

a fidgety semicircle. "What you doin' here by your lonesome? Lost?"

I appear at ease. "No. I'm just out for a walk. What are you guys up to?"

They exchange smirks. They are up to no good. "What's your name?" the leader asks.

"Alisa. What's yours?"

He grins like the young god he thinks he is. "Paul. Hey, you's one beautiful woman, Alisa, you know that? And I appreciate beauty when I see it."

"I bet you do, Paul. Do you appreciate danger when you see it, too?"

They cackle. I am funny, they think. Paul slaps his leg as he laughs. "Are you saying you're dangerous, Alisa?" he asks. "You look like a party babe to me. Me and my stooges, we're going to a party right now. You want to come? It's goin' to be hot."

I consider. "Are you three the only ones going to this party?"

Paul likes it that I'm sharp. "Maybe. But maybe that's all you need." He takes a step closer. There is alcohol on his breath—a Coors beer—Marlboro cigarettes in his coat pocket close to his gun. A brave boy, he puts his right hand on my left shoulder, and his grin is now more of a leer. He adds, "Or maybe all you need is me, babe. What do you say? Want to party?"

I look him in the eye. "No."

He blinks suddenly. My gaze has been known to burn mortal pupils when I give it free rein. But I have held something in check for Paul, and so he is intrigued, not scared. He continues to hold on to my shoulder.

"You don't want to go sayin' no to me, honey. I don't like that word."

"Really."

He glances back at his friends and then nods gravely in my direction. "You don't look like you's from around here. But around here, there's two ways to party. You either do it with a smile on your face or you do it screaming. You know what I mean, Alisa?"

I smile, finally. "Are you going to rape me, Paul?"

He shrugs. "It's up to you, honeysuckle." He draws his piece from his coat, a Smith & Wesson .45 revolver that he probably got for his last birthday. He presses the muzzle beneath my chin. "And it's up to Colleen."

"You call your gun Colleen?"

He nods seriously. "She's a lady. Never lets me down."

My smile grows. "Paul, you are such a simpleton. You can't rape me. Put it out of your mind if you want to be alive come Christmas Day. It's just not going to happen."

My boldness surprises him, angers him. But he quickly grins because his friends are watching and he has to be cool and in control. He presses the gun deeper into my neck, trying to force my head back. But, of course, I don't move an inch, and this confuses him as much as my casual tone.

"You tell me why I can't just have you right now?" he asks. "You tell me, Alisa. Huh? Before I blow your goddamn head off."

"Because I'm armed as well, Paul."

He blinks—my gaze is beginning to fry his brain. "What you got?"

"A knife. A very sharp knife. Do you want to see it?"

He takes a step back, letting go of me, and levels the gun at my belly. "Show it to me," he orders.

I raise my right leg in front of him. My balance is as solid as that of a marble statue. "It's under my pant leg. Take it out and maybe we can have a little duel."

Acting like a stud, throwing his pals a lecherous glance, Paul cautiously reaches up inside my pant leg. Throughout the act, he doesn't realize how close he is to having his head removed by my right foot. But I have compassion, and I don't like to drink from a gusher—it might stain my clothes. Paul's eyes widen as he feels the knife and quickly pulls it free from the leather strap. He handles it lovingly, showing his friends. I wait, acting impatient.

"I want it back," I say finally. "We cannot duel if you hold both weapons."

Paul can't believe me. He is tired of my insolent manner. I begin to tire of him as well. "You's a smart-mouthed bitch. Why should I give you this knife? You might stick it in me while I'm lovin' you."

I nod. "Oh, I'm going to stick it in you, be sure of that. I don't mind that you and your buddies prowl these streets like hungry panthers. This is a jungle and only the strong survive. I understand that, better than you can imagine. But even the jungle has rules. Don't take what you don't need, and if you do, be a sportsman about it. But you're not a sportsman, Paul. You have taken my knife and I want it back. Give it to me right now or you will suffer unpleasantly." I stick out my hand and add in a voice as dark as my long life, "Very unpleasantly."

His anger shows; his cheeks darken with blood. He is not a true animal of the jungle, or he would recognize a poisonous snake when he saw it. He is a coward. Rather than hand over my knife, he tries to slash my open palm with it. Of course he misses because my hand is no longer where it was an instant before. I have withdrawn it to my side, at the same time launching my left foot at his gun. I hit only the revolver, not his hand, and see what the other three don't—the weapon landing on the roof of a three-story apartment complex off to one side. Paul's buddies back up, but he continues looking for his gun. His mouth works, but words are slow to form.

"Huh?" he finally says.

I reach out and grab him by the hair, pulling him close, my left hand closing on his hand that holds my knife. Now he feels my gaze as beamed through a magnifying glass set in the hot sun. He trembles in my grip, and for the first time he must realize how many different kinds of animals are in the jungle. I lean close to his ear and speak softly.

"I see that you have killed before, Paul. That's OK—I have killed, too, many times. I am much older than I look, and as you now know, I am also much stronger. I am going to kill you, but before I do I want to know if you have any final requests. Tell me quick, I'm in a hurry."

He turns his head away, but his eyes cannot escape mine. He tries to pull away and finds we are momentarily welded together. Sweat drips from his face like the river of tears the families of his victims have shed. His partners back farther away. Paul's lower lip trembles.

"Who are you?" he gasps.

I smile. "I'm a party girl, like you said." I lose my smile. "No final requests? Too bad. Say goodbye to mortality. Say hello to the devil for me. Tell him I'll be there soon, to join you."

My words, a poor joke to torment a victim I care nothing for. Yet there is a grain of truth in them. I feel a wave of pain in my chest as I pull Paul closer. It is from the wound when a stake impaled me the night Yaksha perished, a wound that never really healed. Since that night, six weeks earlier, I have never been totally free of pain. And I have begun to suspect I never will be. The full extent of the anguish comes upon me at unexpected moments, fiery waves that roll up like lava. I gag and have to bend over and close my eyes. I have suffered a hundred serious injuries in my fifty centuries, I tell myself. Why does this one not leave me in peace? Truly, a life in constant pain is the life of the damned.

Yet I did not disobey Krishna when I made Ray— not really, I try to convince myself.

Even Yaksha believed I still had the Lord's grace.

"Oh, God," I whisper and clench Paul's blood-filled body to me as if it were a bandage that could seal my invisible scar. I feel myself begin to faint, but just when I feel I can take no more of the surging pain, I hear footsteps in the distance. Quick-sounding footsteps, moving with the speed and power of an immortal. The shock of this realization is like cold water on my burning agony. There is another vampire nearby! I jerk upright, open my eyes. Paul's buddies are fifty feet away and still backing up. Paul looks at me as if he is staring into his own coffin.

"I didn't mean to hurt you, Alisa," he mumbles.

I suck in a deep breath, my heartbeat roaring in my ears. "Yes, you did," I reply and slam the knife down into his right thigh, just above the knee. The blade goes in cleanly, and the tip comes out red and dripping on the other side. An expression of pure horror grips his face, but I have no more time for his excuses. I have bigger game to bag. As I let go of him, he falls to the ground like a trash can that has been kicked over. Turning, I run in the direction of the immortal's footsteps. I leave my knife behind for Paul to enjoy.

The person is a quarter mile away, on the rooftops, leaping from building to building. I cut the distance in half before leaping onto the roofs myself, getting above the three stories in two long steps. Dashing between shattered chimneys and rusty fans, I catch a glimpse of my quarry—a twenty-year-old African-American male youth with muscles bulky enough to squash TVs. Yet a vampire's strength has little to

9

do with this muscle power. Power is related to the purity of the blood, the intensity of the soul, the length of the life. I, who was created at the dawn of civilization by Yaksha, the first of the vampires, am exceptionally strong. Leaping through the air, I know I can catch the other vampire in a matter of seconds. Yet I hold back on purpose. I wish to see where he leads me.

That my prey is indeed a vampire I don't doubt for a second. His every movement matches those of a newborn blood sucker. Also, vampires emit a very subtle fragrance, the faint odor of snake venom, and the soul who runs before me smells like a huge black serpent. The smell is not unpleasant, rather intoxicating to most mortals. I have often used it in the past, on lovers and foes alike. Yet I doubt this young man is even aware of it.

But he is aware of me, oh, yes. He doesn't stop to attack, but continues to run away—he is afraid. I ponder this. How does he know my power? Who told him? My questions are all the same. Who made him? It is my hope that he runs to his maker for help. The pain in my chest has subsided, but I am still thirsty, still anxious for the hunt. To a vampire, another vampire's blood can be a special treat, salt and pepper sprinkled on a rare steak. I move forward without fear. If the guy has partners, so be it. I will destroy them all and then fly back to Oregon in my private jet before the sun comes up, my veins and belly full. Briefly I wonder how Ray is doing without me. His adjustment to being a vampire has been long and painful. I know, without me there, he will not feed.

I hear an ice-cream truck nearby.

In the middle of the night. Odd.

My prey comes to the end of the row of apartment buildings and leaps to the ground with one long flying stride. He stumbles as he contacts the earth. I could take this opportunity to land on his back and break every bone in his spine, but I let him continue on his way. I now know where he is headed—Exposition Park, the home of L.A.'s museums, Memorial Sports Arena, and Memorial Coliseum. It is the Coliseum, where the 1984 Olympics were held, that I guess, is his ultimate destination. He speeds across the vacant parking lot like the Roadrunner in the cartoon. It is lucky there are no mortals standing around to watch me chase him because I am the Coyote, and this is not Saturday morning TV. I am going to catch him, and there will be little of him left when I am done.

The tall fence surrounding the Coliseum is already broken open, and this fact slows me slightly. Briefly I reconsider my boldness. I can easily handle five or six vampires such as the guy I am chasing, but not a dozen, certainly not a hundred. And how many there are, I really don't know. For me the Coliseum may turn out to be like the one in ancient Rome. Yet I am a gladiator at heart, and although I enter the Coliseum cautiously, I do not stop.

I am inside the structure only two minutes when I smell blood. A moment later I find the mangled body of a security guard. Flies buzz above his ripped-out throat; he has been dead several hours. My prey has slipped from my view, but I follow his movements with my ears. I am on the lower level, in the shadows beneath the stands. He is inside the Coliseum proper, running up the bleachers. My hearing stretches out, an expanding wave of invisible radar, as I stand rock still. There are three other souls in the Coliseum, and none of them is human. I track the steps. They meet together at the north end of the building, speak softly, then fan out to the far corners. I doubt that they know my exact whereabouts, but their plan is clear. They wish to surround me, come at me from every direction. I don't wish to disappoint them.

Leaving my shelter, I stride openly down a concrete tunnel and out onto the field, where the moon shimmers on the grass like radioactivity on an atomic blast sight. I see the four vampires at the same time they see me. They pause as I hurry to the fifty-yard line. Let them come to me, I think. I want time to observe them, see if they have weapons. A bullet in the brain, a knife in the heart, might kill me, although the wooden stake through my chest did not, six weeks ago. The pain awakens with the memory, but I will it away. These four are my problem now.

The moon is almost straight overhead. Three vampires continue to move to their corners; the one at the north end is in place and stands motionless, watching me. He is the only Caucasian, tall, thin, his bony hands like a fossilized skeleton. Even in the silver light, in the distance, I note the startling green of his eyes, the bloodshot veins that surround his glowing pupils like the strings of a red-stained spiderweb. He is the leader, and the cocky smile on his acne-scarred face reveals his confidence. He is thirty, maybe, but he will get no older, because I believe he is about to die. He is the one I wish to question, to drink from. I think of the security guard, the girl in the morning's paper. I will kill him slowly and enjoy it.

None of them appears to carry any weapons, but I look around for one for myself, regretting the loss of my knife, which I can fling over a quarter of a mile with deadly accuracy. It is mid-December, as I have said, but I see a collection of track and field equipment at the side of the field. The person in charge of equipment must have forgotten to put it away. I note the presence of a javelin. As the leader studies me, I move casually in the direction of the equipment. But he is sharp, this cold, ugly man, and he knows what I am going for. With a hand movement he signals to his partners to start toward me.

The three dark figures move quickly down the steps. In seconds they have cleared the bleachers and leaped onto the track that surrounds the field. But in those seconds I have reached the equipment and lifted the javelin in my right hand. It is a pity there is only one spear. I raise my empty left hand in the direction of the leader, still far away at the top of the bleachers.

"I would like to talk," I call. "But I am fully capable of defending myself."

The smile on the leader's face, over two hundred yards away, broadens. His goons also grin, although not with the same confidence. They know I am a vampire. They eye the javelin and wonder what I will do with it, such silly young immortals. I keep an eye on all three of them, although I continue to face in the direction of the leader.

"It is always a mistake to decide to die hastily," I call.

The leader reaches behind and removes a knife from his back pocket. There is fresh blood on the tip, I see. I am not worried that he can hit me from such a distance since my ability with my knife has only come after centuries of practice. Yet he handles the weapon skillfully, balancing it in his open palm. The young man whom I chased into the Coliseum is in front of me, between me and the leader. Four against one, I think. I will improve the odds. In a move too swift for mortal eyes to follow, I launch my javelin toward the young man. Too late he realizes my strength and agility. He tries to jump aside but the tip catches him square in the chest, going through his rib cage and spine. I hear the blood explode in his ruptured heart. A death grunt escapes his lip as he topples, the long sharp object sticking through his body.

I hear the whistle of a flying blade.

Too late I realize the skill of the leader.

I dodge to the left, fast enough to save my own heart but not fast enough to avoid having the knife planted in my right shoulder near my arm socket—up to the hilt. The pain is immense, and a wave of weakness shakes my limbs. Without wanting to, I fall to my knees, reaching up to pull out the blade. The other two run toward me at high speed, and I know it will be a matter of seconds before they are on me. Taking his time, the leader begins to descend the steps of the bleachers. I realize that the knife I have in me is my *own*. Obviously the leader observed my little episode with Paul, and yet had time to relieve him of my knife and be here to meet me at the Coliseum. How powerful is he? Can I, wounded as I already am, handle him?

I suspect Paul is no longer suffering any pain from his leg wound.

The other two vampires, not the leader, are my immediate problem. I manage to pull the knife free just as the first one lowers his head to ram me. In a slashing motion I let fly my blade and watch as it goes deep into the top of the man's cranium. Yet I am too weak to dodge aside, and although already dead, he strikes me and knocks me over. I hit the ground hard, two hundred pounds of human meat on top of me. Blood pours over my side from a severed artery deep in my shoulder and for a moment I fear I will pass out. But I do not lie down easily, not while an enemy still stands. I shake off the dead vampire as the third one raises a foot to stomp my face. This one lacks speed, however, and I am able to avoid the blow. Still on the ground, rolling in my own blood; I lash out with my left foot and catch his right shin below the knee, breaking the bone. He lets out a cry and falls, and I am on him in an instant, pinning his massive black arms to the grass carpet with my knees. In the distance I see the leader continue to approach slowly, still confident I will be there, easy prey. For the first time I wonder if I should stay around. I have no time to question the vampire below me at length, as I would like to. I grab his hair, pulling at the roots.

"Who is your leader?" I demand. "What's his name?"

He cannot be more than twenty-five and have been a vampire for longer than a month. A babe in the woods. He doesn't realize the full extent of his peril, even after having seen what I did to his friends. He sneers at me and I believe he will have a short experience at immortality.

"Go to hell, bitch," he says.

"Later," I reply. Had the situation been different I would have reasoned with him, tortured him. Instead I wrap my hands around his neck, and before he can cry out, I twist his head all the way around, breaking every bone in his neck. He goes lifeless beneath me. The next moment I am up and removing my knife from the skull of victim number two. The leader sees me grasp the weapon, but neither accelerates nor slows his approach. His expression is an odd mixture of detachment and eagerness. Indeed, only fifty yards from me now, he looks like a neon nutcase. Well, I think, he will be a dead nut in a moment. Placing the knife in my left palm, I cock my arm and let the blade fly, aiming directly for his heart, as he aimed for mine. I know that I will not miss.

And I don't, in a sense. But I do.

He *catches* the knife in midair, inches from his chest.

He catches it by the handle, something even I could not do.

"Oh, no," I whisper. The guy has the power of Yaksha.

I don't suppose he wants to talk out our difficulties.

Turning, I bolt for the tunnel through which I entered the field. My shoulder throbs, my heart pounds. Each step I take I feel will be my last. The knife will come hurtling again, cut me between the shoulder blades, plunge deep into my heart, which has already been so badly injured. Maybe it will be for the best. Maybe then the pain will finally stop. But, in my heart, I don't want it to stop. Because the pain at least makes me know that I am alive, and I cherish my life above all things, even if I do sometimes take life casually from others. And if I do die, before *he* dies, what will become of life on earth? No question. I know this guy is bad news.

Yet he does not cut me down. He does not, however, let me go, either. I hear him accelerate behind me, and I understand he wants to talk to me—under his own terms—before he drinks my blood. He wants to suck away all my power and feel me die in his arms. But that, I swear, is a privilege he will not have.

Running down the long concrete tunnel, my boots pound like machine gun bullets, his steps like burning tracers behind me, closing, yard by yard. I simply do not have the strength to outrun him. Yet it is not my intention to try. After killing the security guard, these brothers of the night did not bother to remove the man's revolver. Entering the Coliseum, overconfident in my invincibility, I didn't either. But now that gun is my last hope. If I can get to it before my assailant gets to me, I can teach him what it is like to bleed from terrible wounds. I am not large, only ninety-eight

17

pounds naked, and I have already lost at least two pints of blood. Desperately I need to stop, to catch my breath and heal. The security guard's gun can give me that opportunity.

I reach the corpse with the monster only a hundred feet behind me. In a flash he realizes my plan. As I pull the revolver free of its holster, out the corner of my eye I see the powerful vampire wind up with the knife. He will use it now, and not care if he spills what is left of my blood. He must know how difficult bullets are to catch, to dodge, especially when fired by another vampire. Yet I still hope to dodge this knife throw. Gripping the gun firmly, I leap up as I pivot, flying high into the air. Unfortunately, my maneuver does not catch him by surprise. As I open fire, his knife, *my* knife, for the second time, plunges into my body, into my abdomen, near my belly button. It hurts. God, I cannot believe how unlucky I am. Yet there is a chance I can survive, and his good fortune is surely over. While coming down from my leap, I open fire, hitting him as best I can even though he jerks to avoid a fatal wound. I put a bullet in his stomach, one in his neck, his left shoulder, two in his chest. As I hit the ground, I expect him to hit the ground.

But he doesn't. Although staggering, he remains on his feet.

"Oh, Christ," I whisper as I fall to my knees. Will this bastard not die? Across the black shadows of the underbelly of the bleachers, we stare at each other, both bleeding profusely. For a moment our eyes lock, and more than ever I sense the disturbance in him, a vision of reality that no human or vampire should want to share. I am out of bullets. He seems to smile—I don't know what he finds so amusing. Then he turns and shuffles away, and I cannot see him or hear him. Pulling the knife from my naked belly, I swoon on the ground, trying to breathe through a haze of red agony. I honestly cannot remember the last time I had such a bad night.

Still, I am Sita from the dawn of humanity, a vampire of incomparable resiliency—unless, of course, I am to be compared to him, this fiend whose name I still do not know. He is not dead, I am sure of it. And after maybe twenty minutes of writhing on the concrete, I know I will survive. Finally my wounds begin to close and I am able to sit up and draw in a deep breath. Before taking the stake through the heart, my wounds would have closed in two minutes.

"I must be getting old," I mutter.

I cannot hear any vampires in the vicinity. But police are closing in on the Coliseum. After putting my knife back in its proper place under my pant leg, I stumble back up the concrete tunnel and onto the field. I find a hose and wash off as much blood as possible. My shoulder, my belly—they are not scarred. Yet I have lost much blood and am terribly weak, and now I have to worry about the police. Their cruisers park outside the arena. Somebody must have called about the gunshots. With so many bodies lying around, it would be a mistake to be caught inside the Coliseum. I would be taken downtown for question-ing, where my messy clothes would be difficult to explain. I wonder if I should hide inside until things cool off, but, no, that might take hours, if not days, and I am anxious to return home and speak to Ray to figure out what to do next.

But before I leave the arena, I check on the three vampires to make sure they are indeed dead. It is always possible, despite the severity of their wounds, that they could heal and rise again. To be doubly sure, I crack each of their skulls with the heel of my right boot. The grotesque acts cause me no qualms of conscience. I am, after all, just protecting the officers who might find them.

I hurry in the direction of the least amount of noise and am outside, over the fence, and in the parking lot when a bright searchlight suddenly focuses on me. It is from a cruiser, damn. It pulls up alongside me, and a cop who looks as if he has been eating doughnuts for the last twenty years sticks his head out the passenger side.

"What are you doing here at this time of night, young lady?" he asks.

I appear anxious. "I'm trying to find my car. It broke down about an hour ago and I went looking for help and these boys started chasing me. They threw water balloons at me and threatened me." I shiver, catching his eye, pressing his belief buttons. "But I managed to get away."

The cop looks me over from head to foot, but I doubt he notices the bloodstains on my clothes. In the dark they would be hard to see on black clothes. Plus my gaze has shriveled his will. He is swayed by my great beauty, my obvious youth, my long blond hair, which I have let down. He throws his partner behind the wheel a look, then turns back to me and smiles.

"You're lucky all they threw was water balloons," he says. "This is no area to be walking alone at night. Hop in the back and we'll take you back to your car."

It will appear odd to decline the offer. "Thank you," I say, reaching for the door. I climb in the rear seat of the patrol car. His partner, a younger man, glances back at me.

"Were you inside the Coliseum just now?" he asks.

I catch his eye as well. "No," I say clearly. "How could I possibly be in the Coliseum? The fence is fifteen feet high."

He nods like a puppet. "We've just had some trouble in the area is all."

"I understand," I say.

A man calls on their radio. The fat officer explains how they ran into me. The man on the other end is not impressed with my story. He orders them to hold me until he arrives. There is strength in the man's voice, even over the staticky line. I wonder if I will be able to control him as easily as the other two. We sit and wait for the boss to arrive; the officers apologize for the delay. I consider drinking both officers' blood and leaving them dazed and incoherent, but I've always had a thing for cops. The fat one offers me a doughnut, which does little to satisfy my deeper hunger.

The man who arrives is not LAPD but FBI. He pulls up alone in an unmarked car, and I am told to get in up front. I do not resist. He introduces himself as Special Agent Joel Drake, and he has an aura of authority about him. A young man, he has blond hair almost as light as my own, and blue eyes as well, although these are darker than mine. He wears a sea blue sport coat, expensive white slacks. He is strikingly handsome. I feel, as I climb in beside him, like an actor in a series. *Agent Vampire*—there should be such a show. His face is tan, his features sharp and intelligent. He studies me in the dome light before shutting his door. He notices that I am soaking wet, although, once again, the bloodstains on my black outfit are all but invisible. The other officers drive off.

"What's your name?" he asks.

"Alisa Perne."

"Where's your car?"

"I don't know exactly. I've been walking for an hour, lost."

"You say you got hit with water balloons thrown at you by a bunch of guys? You expect me to believe that?"

"Yes," I say, and I catch his eye, such beautiful eyes really. I hesitate to blunt his will too forcibly, afraid it might damage him. Yet he is strong; he will not be moved without great power. Nevertheless, I cannot let him take me in for questioning. Lowering my voice, I pitch my tone in such a manner that he will feel as if I am speaking between his ears, as if he were in fact thinking what I am saying.

"I have done nothing wrong," I say gently. "Everything I tell you is true. I am a young woman, helpless, a stranger here. The best thing you can do is take me to my car."

He considers what I say for several seconds. I know my voice runs like an echo inside him. Then he shakes himself, seemingly throwing off my implant. I can sense his emotions, although I cannot read his thoughts. His doubt remains strong. He reaches out and shuts his door; the engine is already running.

"Have you been inside the Coliseum tonight?" he asks.

"No. What's inside the Coliseum?"

"Never mind. The police say they found you here, in the parking lot. What were you doing here?"

"Fleeing from the guys who harassed me."

"How many were there?"

"I'm not sure. Three or four."

"We have a report from two young men in the area. They say their buddy was attacked by someone who fits your description. Minutes ago we found their buddy's body, lying in a gutter. What do you have to say about that?"

I grimace. "I know nothing about it. How did he die?"

Joel frowns. "Violently."

I shake my head, looking anxious. "I was just trying to get back to my car. Can't you take me there? It's been a long night for me."

"Where are you from?"

"Oregon. I don't know L.A. I took a wrong exit and then my car stalled. But with your help, I might be able to find it." I reach over and touch his arm, holding his eyes once more, but softly, without fire. "Please?" I say.

He nods finally and puts the car in gear. "Which exit did you get off?"

"I forget the name. It's up here. I can show you, and maybe we can retrace my steps." I point as we pull out of the parking lot and head north in the direction of the freeway. "Honestly, I've never hurt anyone in my life."

He chuckles bitterly. "I don't imagine you had anything to do with what happened tonight."

"I've heard L.A.'s a violent town."

He nods grimly. "Especially lately. I suppose you've read the papers?"

"Yes. Are you in charge of the murder investigation?"

"Several of us are overseeing it."

"Have you any leads?"

"No. But that's off the record."

I smile. "I'm not a reporter, Agent Drake."

He smiles faintly. "You shouldn't get within twenty miles of this area at night. How long are you going to be in L.A.?"

"Why?"

"We might need to ask you more questions later."

"I'll be around. I can give you a number once we find my car."

"That's fine. Did you get off the Harbor Freeway or the Santa Monica?"

"I was on the Santa Monica Freeway. Let's continue north a few blocks. I think I'll recognize the right street."

"How old are you Alisa?"

"Twenty-two."

"What's your business in L.A.?"

"I'm visiting friends. I'm thinking of going to school here next year."

"Oh. Where?"

"USC."

"The Coliseum is right next to USC."

"That's the reason I was driving around here. One of my friends lives on campus." I shiver again. "But with all this violence I'm seriously reconsidering my choice of universities."

"That's understandable." He glances over, checking out my body this time. He does not wear a wedding ring. "So you're a student. What are you majoring in?"

"History," I say.

We drive without talking for a few minutes, me merely pointing where I think we should turn next. Actually, I do not want to take him to my car because even though he is responding to my suggestions, he still has a will of his own. And he is obviously highly trained. He would memorize my license plate number if I brought him to my rental. A block from where I have parked, passing a red Honda, I signal for him to stop.

"This is it," I say, opening the car door. "Thank you so much."

"Do you think it will start now?" he asks.

"Why don't you pull in front of me and wait to see if I can get it started." I add, a sexy note in my voice, "Could you do that for me?"

"No problem. Alisa, do you have any ID on you?"

I grin foolishly. "I knew you were going to ask that. I'm afraid I'm driving without my license. But I can give you a number where I'll be tomorrow. It's 310-555-4141. This is a genuine L.A. number that will ring through to my house in Oregon. You can call me there any time for the next three days. Do you want me to write the number down for you?"

He hesitates, but I know he is thinking that with my license plate number he can always trace me. "That's not necessary, it's an easy number to remember." He pauses again, studying the damp marks on my shirt. There is no way he can tell they're bloodstains just by looking at them, but I have to wonder if he can smell the odor, even after my heavy washing. Despite my subtle influence, he would never let me go if he definitely saw blood. And I am not free yet. "Can you give me an address as well?" he asks.

"Joel," I say in my special way. "You don't really think I killed anyone, do you?"

He backs away slightly. "No."

"Then why do you want all these things from me?"

He hesitates, shrugs. "If you have an address, I will take it. Otherwise your phone number is enough for me for now." He adds, "We'll probably talk tomorrow."

"Good enough. It was nice meeting you." I step out of his car. "Now I just hope the damn thing starts."

Joel pulls in front of me and waits, as I suggested. It was not a suggestion I made willingly, but felt I needed to allay his suspicions. The Honda door is locked, but I open it with a hard yank and slip behind the wheel. With two fingers I break the ignition switch, noting how Joel studies my license plate number in his rearview mirror. He writes it down as I press the contact wires together and the engine turns over. I wave as I quickly pull away from the curb. I don't want the people in the adjacent house to hear me leaving with their car. After driving around the block, I get into my own car, and in less than an hour I am in the air, flying in my personal Learjet toward Oregon. Yet I know I will return to Los Angeles soon to finish the war with the powerful vampire.

For good or evil.

2

Ray is not home when I get there. Our residence is new, obviously, since my original house blew up with Yaksha inside. Our modern mansion in the woods is not far from the old house. It has many electronic conveniences, a view of the ocean, and heavy drapes to block out the midday sun. More than any other vampire I have known, Ray is the most excruciatingly sensitive to the sun. He is made like a Bram Stoker model vampire out of old legends. Many things about his new existence trouble him. He misses his school friends, his old girlfriend, and especially his father. But I can give him none of these things—certainly not his father, since it was I who killed the man. I can only give him my love, which I dreamed would be enough.

I am only in the house two minutes before I am back in my car looking for him. Dawn is an hour away.

I find him sitting on his ex-lover's porch, but Pat McQueen is unaware of his nearness. Along with her parents, she is sleeping inside. I know she thinks Ray perished in the blast that supposedly took my life, too. He sits with his head buried in his knees and doesn't even bother to look up as I approach. I let out a sigh.

"What if I was a cop?" I ask.

He looks up, his melancholy consuming his beauty. Yet my heart aches to see him again; it has ached ever since he entered my life, both the physical heart and the emotional one. Radha, Krishna's friend, once told me that longing is older than love, and that one cannot exist without the other. Her name, in fact, meant longing, and Krishna's meant love. But I never saw how their relationship tortured them the way my passion for Ray does me. I have given him the kingdom of eternal night, and all he wants to do is take a walk under the sun. I note his weakness, his hunger. Six weeks and I am still forcing him to feed, even though we don't harm or kill our meals. He doesn't look happy to see me, and that saddens me more.

"If you were a cop," he says, "I could easily disarm you."

"And create a scene doing it."

He nods to the blood on my top. "It looks as if you have created a scene or two tonight." When I don't respond, he adds, "How was Los Angeles?"

"I'll tell you back at the house." I turn. "Come."

"No."

I stop, glance back over my shoulder. "The sun will be up soon."

"I don't care."

"You will when you see it." He doesn't answer me. I go and sit beside him, put my arm around his shoulder. "Is it Pat? You can talk to her, you know, if you must. I just think it's a bad idea."

He shakes his head. "I cannot talk to her."

"Then what are you doing here?"

He stares at me. "I come here because I have nowhere else to grieve."

"Ray."

"I mean, I don't know where my father's buried." He turns away and shrugs. "It doesn't matter. It's all gone."

I take his hand; he barely lets me. "I can take you to where I buried your father. But it's just a hole in the ground, covered over. It will not help you."

He looks up at the stars. "Do you think there are vampires on other planets?"

"I don't know. Maybe. In some distant galaxy there might be a whole planet filled with vampires. This planet almost was."

He nods. "Except for Krishna."

"Yes. Except for him."

He continues to stare at the sky. "If there were such a planet, where there were only vampires, it would not survive long. They would destroy one another." He looks at me. "Do I do that to you? Destroy you?"

I shake my head sadly. "No. You give me a great deal. I just wish I knew what to give you in return, to help you forget."

He smiles gently. "I don't want to forget, Sita. And maybe that is my problem." He pauses. "Take me to his grave. We won't stay long."

"Are you sure?"

"Yes."

I stand, offer him my hand. "Very well."

We drive into the woods. I lead him through the trees. I remember the spot where I buried P.I. Michael Riley, of course—I remember everything. Also, I smell the faint fumes of his decaying body as they seep up from beneath six feet of earth. I fear Ray smells them as well. The life of a vampire is a life of many corpses; they do not invoke in me the strong emotions they do in most humans. Ray drops to his knees as we reach the spot, and I retreat a few dozen feet because I want him to be alone with his emotions—a caldron of sorrows. I am still too weak to let them wash over me. Or else I am too guilty. I hear Ray weep dry tears on a missing tombstone.

My two most recent wounds have completely healed, but my chest continues to burn. I remember the night Ray pulled the stake from my heart while my house burned nearby. Barely conscious, I didn't know if I would live or die, and for the next three days Ray didn't, either. Because even though my wound closed quickly, I remained unconscious. All that time I had the most extraordinary dream.

I was in a starship flying through space. Ray was beside me and our destination was the Pleiades star cluster, the Seven Sisters, as it is often called by astronomers. Outside our forward portals, we could see the blue-white stars growing steadily in size and brilliance, and although our journey was long, we were filled with excitement the whole time. Because we knew we were finally returning home to where we belonged, where we weren't vampires, but angels of light who lived on the radiance of the stars alone. The dream was painful to awaken from, and I still pray each time I lie down to sleep that it will return. The color of the stars reminded me of Krishna's eyes.

Ray spills his grief quickly. We are back in the car and headed for home as the eastern sky begins to lighten. My lover sits silently beside me, staring at nothing, and my own dark thoughts keep my lips closed. My energy is at a low, but I know I mustn't rest, not until I have formulated a plan to stop the black plague spreading six hundred miles south of us. He of the wicked eyes will make more vampires the next night, I know. Replacements for the ones I destroyed. And they in turn will make their own. Each day, each hour, is crucial. The human race is in danger. Krishna, I pray, give me the strength to destroy this enemy. Give me the strength not to destroy myself.

As Ray lies down to rest, I let him drink from my veins, a little, enough to get him through the day. Even that mouthful drains me more. Yet I do not lie down beside him as he closes his eyes to sleep. Let him dream of his father, I think. I will tell him of Los Angeles later.

I visit my friend Seymour Dorsten. Twice I have seen him since I destroyed the AIDS virus in his blood with a few drops of mine. His health is greatly improved. He has a girlfriend now and I tell him I am jealous, but he doesn't believe me. I climb in his window and wake him by shoving him off his bed and onto the floor. He grins as his head contacts the hard wood with a loud thud. Only my Seymour would welcome such treatment.

"I was dreaming about you," he says, his blankets half covering his face.

"Did I have my clothes on?" I ask.

"Of course not." He sits up and rubs the back of his head. "What the eyes have seen, the mind cannot forget."

"When did you ever see me naked?" I ask, although I know the answer.

He chuckles in response. I do not fool him, Seymour the Great, my personal biographer. Knowing our psychic bond, I wonder if he has spent the night writing about my trials, but he shakes his head when I ask. He watched a video with his new girl and went to bed early.

I tell him about Los Angeles, why I am bloody.

"Wow," he says when I am done.

I lean back on his bed, resting my back against the wall. He continues to sit on the floor. "You're going to have to do better than that," I say.

He nods. "You want me to help you figure out where they're coming from."

"They're coming from that monster. I have no doubt about that. I want to know where he came from." I shake my head. "I thought about it all the way here, and I have no explanation."

"There is always an explanation. Do you remember the famous Sherlock Holmes quote? 'When you have eliminated the impossible, whatever remains, no matter how improbable, must be the truth.'" Seymour thinks, his palms pressed together. "A vampire that strong could only have been created by Yaksha."

"Yaksha is dead. Also, Yaksha would not have created a vampire. He was bound by the vow he made to Krishna. He spent the last five thousand years destroying them."

"How do you know Yaksha is dead? Maybe he survived the blast."

"Highly unlikely."

"But not impossible. That's my point. Yaksha was the only one besides you who could make another vampire. Unless you want to bring in the possibility that another yakshini has been accidentally invoked into the corpse of a pregnant woman."

"Don't remind me of that night," I growl.

"You're in a bad mood. But I suppose being stabbed twice in the same night, with your own knife, would do that to anybody."

I smile thinly. "Are you making fun of me? You know, I'm thirsty. I could open your veins right now and drink my fill and there would be nothing you could do about it."

Seymour is interested. "Sounds kinky. Should I take off my clothes?"

I throw a pillow at him, hard. It almost takes off his head. "Haven't you been able to get that girl of yours into bed? What's wrong with you? With my blood in your veins, you should be able to have who you want when you want."

He rubs his head again, probably thinking it is going to be sore for the rest of the day. "How do you know I haven't slept with her yet?"

"I can spot a male virgin a mile away. They walk like they've been riding a horse too long. Let's return to our problem. Yaksha would not have made this guy. It's out of the question. Yet you are right—Yaksha is the only one who could have made him. A paradox. How do I solve it? And how do I destroy this creature that clearly has at least twice my strength and speed? Tell me, young author, and I might let you live long enough to enjoy carnal pleasure with this silly girl you have foolishly chosen over me."

"I'm sorry, I can't answer your questions. But I can tell you where you must look to find the answers."

"Where?"

"Where you left the trail last. Where you last saw Yaksha. He went up in the blast you set at your house, but even dynamite leaves remains. Find out what became of those remains, and you might find out how your new enemy came to be."

I nod. His reasoning is sound, as always. "But even if I learn how he came to be, I still have to learn how to destroy him."

"You will. Yaksha was a more difficult foe. He knew at least as much as you about what a vampire could or could not do. The way this guy is carrying on, he must be newborn. He is still learning what he is. He doesn't know where he is weak. Find him, strike at that weak point, and he will fall."

I slip down onto the floor and kneel to kiss Seymour on the lips. Gently I toss up his hair. "You are so confident in me," I say. "Why is that?"

He starts to say something funny, but his expression falters. He trembles slightly beneath my touch. "Is he really that bad?" he asks softly.

"Yes. You are wrong when you say Yaksha was a more difficult foe. In his own way, Yaksha was a protector of mankind. This guy is a psychopath. He is bent on destroying all humanity. And he could succeed. If I don't stop him soon, nothing will."

"But you saw him only briefly."

"I looked deep into his eyes. I saw enough. Believe what I tell you."

Seymour touches my face, admiration, and love, in his eyes. "I have confidence in you because when you met me I was as good as dead and you saved me. You're the hero in my story. Find him, Sita, corner him. Then kick his ass. It will make for a great sequel." He adds seriously, "God will help you."

I squeeze his hand carefully, feeling once more my weakness, my pain. It will not leave me, I am certain, until I leave this world. The temptation is there before me for the first time. To just run and hide in oblivion. Yet I know I must not, I cannot. Like Yaksha, I have one last duty to perform before I die and return to the starry heaven of my dream.

Or to a cold hell. But I do not like the cold.

No vampire does. Like snakes, it slows us down.

"I fear the devil will help him," I say. "And I'm not sure who's stronger."

3 ~~~

The sun is firmly in the sky as I sit in my office to sort out what to do next. Three types of professionals arrived after my house blew up six weeks earlier: firefighters, police officers, and paramedics. Ray told me this. They didn't talk to Ray, who had dragged me out of sight into the woods, but I contacted them later once I had regained consciousness. I pleaded innocent to any knowledge of the explosion: its cause or the reason it was rigged. At that time they didn't tell me of any human remains found in the vicinity. That, of course, doesn't mean a body wasn't found. The police could have withheld that information from me. For all I know I am still under investigation for the explosion and whatever was discovered in the area.

I need a contact with the local police and I need it immediately. The paramedics and the hospital would have the remains of Yaksha, but if I do not go through the proper channels and authorities, they will show me nothing. With my extensive contacts and wealth, I can develop a contact, but it will take time. As I sit at my desk, thinking, a light on my phone begins to blink. It is an out-of-state call. I pick it up.

"Yes?" I say.

"Alisa?"

"Yes. Agent Joel Drake—how nice of you to call." I make a decision immediately, figuring it is a sign from Krishna that the FBI man has phoned at this precise instant. Of course, I do not believe in signs, I am just desperate. I add, "I've been meaning to call you. There are some things we should discuss that I failed to bring up last night."

He is interested. "Such as?"

"I have a lead on who is behind the murders."

He takes a moment. "Are you serious?"

"Yes. I have a very good lead."

"What is it?"

"I will only tell you in person. Fly into Portland this afternoon and I'll pick you up at the airport. I guarantee you'll be glad you came."

"I thought you said you wouldn't be leaving town for a few days?"

"I lied. Call the airlines. Book your flight."

He chuckles. "Hold on a second. I can't fly up to Oregon in the middle of an investigation. Tell me what you know and then we can talk."

"No," I say firmly. "You must come here."

"Why?"

"The murderer is from here."

"How do you know that?"

I pitch my voice in my most beguiling manner. "I know many things, Agent Drake. That one of the guys you found in the coliseum had a javelin through his chest, the other had his skull stabbed open, and every bone in the neck of the third was shattered. Don't ask me how I know these things and don't tell your FBI pals about me. Not if you want to solve this case *and* get all the credit. Think about it, Joel, you can be the big hero."

My knowledge stuns him. He considers. "You misunderstand me, Alisa. I don't need to be a hero. I just want to stop the killing."

He is being sincere. I like that.

"It will stop if you come here," I say softly.

He closes his eyes; I hear them close. My voice will not leave his mind. He wonders if I am some kind of witch. "Who are you?" he asks.

"It doesn't matter. I will hold while you book your flight. Take the earliest one."

"I will have to tell my partners where I'm going."

"No. Just the two of us are going to work on this. That's my condition."

He chuckles again, this time without mirth. "You're pretty gutsy for a young woman."

I think of the knife that stabbed me in the belly less than twelve hours ago. "I have strong guts," I agree.

Joel puts me on hold. A few minutes later he

returns. His plane will land in three hours. I agree to meet him at the gate. After setting down the phone, I leave my office and crawl into bed beside Ray. He stirs and turns his back to me but doesn't wake. Portland is an hour and a half away. I have only ninety minutes to rest before I must take on the enemy.

Joel looks tired when I pick him up at the airport. I don't imagine he got much sleep the previous night. He immediately starts with his questions, but I ask him to wait until we are in my car. Once inside I put on music, a tape of my playing the piano. We drive toward Mayfair. I am still thinking how I should approach this matter. Since we are dealing with evidence that points toward a mysterious agency, I am not worried about staying conservative.

"Who is the pianist?" he asks finally.

"Do you like it?"

"The music is haunting, and the pianist is wonderful."

An appropriate choice of words. "It's me."

"Are you serious?"

"You have asked me that twice today. I am always serious, Agent Drake."

"Joel, please. Is Alisa your real name?"

"Why? Have you been researching me?"

"A bit. I haven't turned up much."

"You mean, you haven't turned up an Alisa Perne in your computers?"

"That's correct. What's your real name and who taught you to play such exquisite piano?"

"I am self-taught. And I like to be called Alisa."

"You haven't answered my question."

"I answered one of them."

He stares at me. For a few sentences I forgot to be careful how I pitched my voice, and the echo of my age creeps into it. My words and voice, I know, can throb like living ghosts. My music is not the only thing that is haunting.

"How old did you say you were?" he asks.

"Older than I look. You want to know how I know about the murders."

"Among other things. You lied to me last night when you said you had not been in the Coliseum."

"That is correct. I was there. I saw the three young men in the field killed."

"Did you get a good look at the killer?"

"Good enough."

He pauses. "Do you know him?"

"No. But he is associated with a man I once knew. That man died in an explosion at my house six weeks ago. The reason I have brought you here is to help me trace the remains of that man. We are driving to the Mayfair Police Station now. I want you to ask them to open their files to you."

He shakes his head. "No way. You're going to answer my questions before I do anything to help you."

"Or you will arrest me?"

"Yes."

I smile thinly. "That will not happen. And I am not going to answer all your questions, just the ones I choose to answer. You have no choice but to cooperate with me. Like you said last night—you have no leads. And you are more in the dark than you admit. You have several people who seem to have been killed by a person of extraordinary strength. A person so strong, in fact, that he seems superhuman."

"I wouldn't go that far."

I snort softly. "It takes a great deal of strength to snap every cervical in a man's neck. Isn't that what the autopsy showed?"

Joel shifts uneasily, but I have his full attention. "The autopsy isn't complete on any of the victims."

"But the LAPD medical examiner has told you about the guy's neck. It makes you wonder, doesn't it?"

He speaks carefully. "Yes. It makes me wonder how you know these things."

I reach over and touch his leg. I have a very sensual touch, when I wish to flaunt it, and I must admit I find myself attracted to Joel. Not that I love him as I do Ray, but I wouldn't mind seducing him, as long as Ray wouldn't know. Having had ten thousand lovers, I don't share most mortals' illusions of the sacredness of fidelity. Yet I will not risk hurting Ray for sex, and I will not lie to him anymore. Joel feels the electricity of my fingers and shifts all the more. I like my boys fidgety.

"You want to say something?" I ask, my hand still on his thigh.

He clears his throat. "You are very alluring, Alisa. Particularly when you are being vague, or trying to be persuasive." He stares down at my hand as if trying to decide whether it is a priceless jewel or a spider that has crawled into his lap. "But I am beginning to see through your facade."

I remove my hand, not insulted. "Is that all it is? A facade?"

He shakes his head. "Where did you grow up?"

I burst out laughing. "In the jungle! A place not unlike where these murders are happening. I watched as that young man's neck was snapped. A normal person couldn't do that. The person you are looking for is not normal. Nor was my friend who died when my house blew up. If we can find what became of him, his remains, then we can find your murderer—I hope. But don't ask me how these people are not normal, how they have such strength, or even why my house was blown up. I won't tell you."

He keeps looking at me. "Are you normal, Alisa?" he asks.

"What do you think?"

"No."

I pat his leg. "It's all right. You go on thinking that way."

Yet, I think, he knows too much about me already.

When all this is over, I am going to have to kill Joel Drake.

4 ~~

On the drive to Mayfair Joel tells me about his life. Maybe I pry the information out of him a bit. Maybe he has nothing to hide. I listen attentively and grow to like him more with each passing mile, much to my disquiet. Maybe that's his intention—to be open with me. Already, I think, he knows I am more dangerous than I appear.

"I grew up on a farm in Kansas. I wanted to be an FBI agent from the first time I saw that old series, *The F.B.I.*, that starred Efrem Zimbalist, Jr. Do you remember that show? It was great. I suppose I did have dreams of being a hero: catching bank robbers, finding kidnapped kids, stopping serial murderers. But when I graduated from the academy in Quantico,

Virginia, I was assigned to blue collar crime in Cedar Rapids, Iowa. I spent twelve months chasing accountants. Then I got a big break. My landlady was murdered. Stabbed with a knife and buried in a cornfield. That was at the end of summer. The local police were called in, and they found the body pretty quick. They were sure her boyfriend did it. They even had the guy arrested and ready to stand trial. But I kept telling them he loved his woman and wouldn't have hurt her for the world. They wouldn't listen to me. There is an old rivalry between the FBI and police. Even in Los Angeles, working on this case, the LAPD constantly withholds information from me.

"Anyway, privately, I went after another suspect—the woman's sixteen-year-old son. I know, he sounds like an unlikely candidate—the woman's only child. But I knew her son as well as the boyfriend, and the kid was bad news. An addict ready to steal the change from a homeless person. I was their tenant and I caught him breaking into my car once to steal my radio. He was into speed. When he was high, he was manic—either the nicest guy in the world or ready to poke your eyes out. He had lost all sense of reality. At his mother's funeral he began to sing "Whole Lot of Love." Yet, at the same time, he was cunning. His bizarre behavior hid his guilt. But I knew he'd done it, and, as you're fond of saying, don't ask me why. There was something in his eyes when I talked to him about his mother—like he was thinking about how nice it was finally to have the house all to himself.

"The problem was, I didn't have a shred of evidence

that linked him to the crime. But I kept watching him, hoping he'd reveal something. I was anxious to move to another place, but during my off hours, I told myself, I was on stakeout. I felt in my gut something would turn up.

"Then Halloween came, and that evening the sonofabitch was out on his front porch carving a huge jack-o'-lantern. He flashed me a nauseatingly sweet smile as I walked to my car, and something about his expression made me pause to look closer at his knife. By this time the victim's boyfriend was in the middle of his trial, and losing. As I mentioned, the woman had been stabbed, and as I studied her son and the pumpkin on his lap, I remembered how the autopsy report noted the unusual spacing of the metal teeth marks on the victim's skin. This knife was weird—the cutting edge had irregularly spaced ridges.

"I hid my interest in the knife with a nonchalant wave, but the next day I got a warrant to search the house. I obtained the knife, and its cutting edge was compared to the photographs taken by the coroner. There was a match. To make a long story short, the son was eventually convicted. He is serving a life sentence in Iowa as we speak." Joel adds, "All because of one jack-o'-lantern."

"All because of one sharp agent," I say. "Was your success on the case your ticket to bigger and better things?"

"Yes. My boss was pleased by my persistence, and I was put on a couple of old unsolved murder cases. I solved one of them and was promoted. I have been working difficult murder cases in L.A. ever since." He nods. "Persistence is the key to solving most mysteries."

"And imagination. Why did you tell me this story?"

He shrugs. "Just trying to make casual conversation with a potential witness."

"Not true. You want to see how I react to your tales of insight and intrigue."

He has to laugh. "What do you want with me, Alisa? To make me into a hero or a goat? I did as you requested—I told no one where I was going. But I'll have to call in some time today. And if I tell them I'm in Oregon riding around with a cute blond, it's not going to look good on my record."

"So you think I'm cute?" I ask.

"You catch the operative words, don't you?"

"Yes." I add, "I think you're cute as well."

"Thank you. Do you have a boyfriend?"

"Yes."

"Is he normal?"

I feel a pang in my chest. "He is wonderful."

"Can he verify where you were the last two days?"

"That's not necessary. I already told you I was in the Coliseum watching necks being broken and chests pierced. If there is guilt by association, then I'm guilty as sin."

"Aren't you worried about telling that to an FBI agent?"

"Do I look worried?"

"No. That's what worries me." His tone becomes

businesslike again. "How did this abnormal person break the young man's neck?"

"With his bare hands."

"But that's impossible."

"I told you not to ask me these questions. Let's wait till we get to Mayfair, see what we find out from the local police. Then perhaps I'll tell you more."

"I will have to call the local office of the FBI and have them notify the police that I'm coming. They won't open their files to me just because I walk in the front door."

I hand him my cellular phone. "Notify whoever you have to, Joel."

The Mayfair police give us scant information, and yet it is crucial. While I wait in the car and listen to the conversation that takes place inside the station, Joel learns that there was a body recovered from the explosion at my house, not just pieces of flesh as I expected. I have to wonder—how did Yaksha's form survive the blast? He was more powerful than any creature that walked the earth, but even he should have had to bow to several crates of dynamite. The police tell Joel that the body was taken to a morgue in Seaside, seventy miles south of Mayfair, the city where I combated the people Yaksha sent after me, Slim and his partners.

"Please! I don't want to die."

"Then you should never have been born."

Slim's blood was bitter tasting, as was his end. So be it.

Joel returns to my car and I give him every chance to lie to me about what the police have told him. But he gives me the straight facts.

"We're going to Seaside," I say, handing him the phone again. "Tell them we're on our way."

"What was the name of your friend who died?"

"Yaksha."

"What kind of name is that?"

"It's Sanskrit." I glance over. "It's the name of a demonic being."

He dials the Seaside morgue. "Love the company you keep."

I can't resist—I give him a wink. "It's improving by the hour."

Joel is big-time FBI. The morgue is only too happy to show him whatever bodies they have on ice. The problem is, when we get there—this time I go inside with Joel—the body we are looking for is missing. Now I know what the Mayfair police were holding back. Joel looks irritated. I feel dizzy. Is Yaksha still alive? Did he create the monster who attacked me? If that is the case, then we are all doomed. Seymour can have all the confidence in the world in me, but I will not be able to stop my creator if he is bent on spreading our black blood. Yet it makes no sense. Yaksha was looking forward to his end, secure in the knowledge that he was going to his death having done the Lord's bidding.

"What do you mean, it's missing?" Joel demands. "What happened to it?"

The bespeckled coroner shakes at Joel's question. He is the kid who has been caught with his fingers in the cookie jar. Only this guy's fingers look as if they have been dipped in formaldehyde every morning for the last twenty years. The jaundice virus could be oozing out of his big ears. Here I am a vampire, but even I can't understand why anyone would want to be a coroner and work with corpses all day, even fresh ones filled with nice blood. Morticians are an even stranger lot. I once buried a mortician alive—in France after World War II—in his most expensive coffin. He made the mistake of saying all Americans were pigs, which annoyed me. He kicked like a pig as I shoveled the dirt on top of him. I enjoy a little mischief.

"We don't know for sure," the coroner replies. "But we believe it was stolen."

"Well, that's just great," Joel growls. "How long was the body here before it disappeared?"

"A week."

"Excuse me," I interrupt. "I am Special Agent Perne and an expert when it comes to forensic evidence. Are you absolutely sure the body we are discussing was in fact a body? That the person was dead?"

The coroner blinks as if he has tissue sample in his eyes. "What are you suggesting?"

"That the guy simply got up and walked out," I say.

"That would have been quite impossible."

"Why?" I ask.

"Both his legs had been blown off," the coroner says. "He was dead. We had him in the freezer all the time he was here."

"Do you know who might have stolen the body?" Joel asks.

The coroner straightens. "Yes. We had an employee here, an Eddie Fender, who vanished the same time as the body. He took off without even collecting his final paycheck. He worked the night shift and was often unsupervised."

"What was his position?" Joel asks.

"He was an orderly, of sorts."

I snort. "He helped prepare the bodies for dissection."

The coroner is insulted. "We do not dissect people, Agent Perne."

Joel raises his hand as a call for peace. "Do you have a résumé on this guy? A job application?"

The coroner nods. "We handed over copies of those items to the Seaside police. But you are welcome to see the originals. If you'll come into my office, I'll dig them out of our files."

"Go ahead," I say to Joel. "I want to browse, check out the sights."

He rolls his eyes. "Don't disturb the dead."

I check the individual freezer lockers in the back. My keen sense of smell brings me quickly to the one Yaksha occupied. The aroma of the venom—still there even in death, in ice. Yet the odor is not precisely as I remember it, even from six weeks or five thousand years ago. There is something wrong with the faint traces of his blood that remain in the cold locker. Somehow it has been polluted. Grotesque vibrations linger over the hollow space. If Yaksha is in fact dead, he did not leave the world thinking about Krishna, as he hoped. My disquiet deepens.

While Joel stays with the coroner, I wander deeper into the morgue and find an office space with a secretary with her feet up on her desk, doing her nails. I like a woman who doesn't take her job too seriously. This gal doesn't even bother to sit up as I walk in. Of course, to some, I look like a teenager. About thirty, she has a *National Enquirer* and a two-liter bottle of Diet Pepsi sitting on her desk beside a computer screen that keeps flashing: TEMPORARY MALFUNCTION! Her lips swim in red paint; her hair stands up like an antique wig. Twenty pounds overweight, she looks jovial, a little slutty.

"Wow," she says when she sees me. "Aren't you a pretty little thing! What are you doing in this haunted house?"

I smile. "I am with Special Agent Joel Drake. My name is Alisa Perne. We are investigating a murder."

Now she sits up. "You're FBI? You look like a cheerleader."

I sit down. "Thank you. You look like an executive secretary."

She pulls out a cigarette and waves her hand. "Yeah, right. And this is the executive suite. What can I do for you?"

"Did you know Eddie Fender?"

"The guy who stole the stiff?"

"Did he steal it?"

She lights her cigarette. "Sure. He was in love with that corpse." She chuckles. "It did more for him than I ever did."

"Did you see Eddie socially?"

She leans forward and blows smoke. "You mean, did I screw him? Listen, sister, I would just as soon blow my brains out as do it with Eddie Fender, if you get my meaning."

I nod. "What's your name?"

"Sally Diedrich. I'm not German, just got the name. Is Eddie a suspect in a murder case?"

"We're just gathering background information at this point. I would appreciate anything you could tell me about him."

Sally whistles. "I could give you background on that guy that would make you want to turn your back and run the other way. Listen, you got a minute? Let me tell you a story about Eddie and his relationship to reality."

I cross my legs. "I have many minutes. Tell me everything you know."

"This happened three months ago. We had a temp in here helping me search through some of our oldest files for missing X rays. Don't believe what the cops and the papers tell you—none of that forensic evidence should hold up in court. We're forever mixing autopsy reports together. We had a dead guy who stayed here a few days, and it says on his death certificate that he croaked because of a tubal pregnancy. Anyway, the temp's name was Heather Longston and she was pretty as pie, if a bit slow. Eddie flirted with her and asked her out, and she said sure before I could warn her. By the time I did talk to her, she felt 'committed.' That's an example of how stupid she was. A guy compliments her on her dress and offers to take her to dinner and she feels committed. Heather was the kind of girl who felt obligated to buy everything that gets sold over the phone. I visited her home once, and she had two sets of those carving knives that they say can be used as dowsing rods to find water and oil.

"So Heather went out with Eddie, and let me tell you, that was one date for Ripley's Believe It or Not! First, he took her to McDonald's for dinner. She told me he had three hamburgers, nothing else. No drink, no fries, no nothing. He ate the hamburgers plain— meat on a bun. Then he took her for a walk. Guess where he took her?"

"The cemetery," I say.

"You got it! He wolfed down his burgers and took her hand and they went tombstone sighting. Heather said he got all giddy when they got to the graves. He wanted to lie down on top of them and make out. Said it would give her a rush like she wouldn't believe. Well, she believed it. They made out six feet above some rotting corpse. Heather said he wasn't a bad kisser. He swiped some flowers off a grave and gave them to her as a present. The gesture touched her, I swear." Sally shook her head. "Isn't it just lovely when two loonies get together?"

"As lovely as when two uglies get together," I say.

"I hear you. Anyway, here comes the sick part. Eddie takes her back to his apartment to watch videos, and guess what he pulls out of his drawer?"

"Pornographic films?"

Sally leans farther forward. Her big breasts crush last week's work and push her bottle of Diet Pepsi aside. "Snuff films. Do you know what those are?"

"Yes. Videos made where people—usually woman—are supposedly killed."

"Sick, huh? Eddie had a whole set of them. He showed Heather three or four—they're usually pretty short, I understand—before she figured out she wasn't watching the latest Disney releases. Then she got up and wanted to leave. The only problem was, Eddie wouldn't let her."

"Did he threaten to harm her?"

Sally scratched her head. "I'm not sure. I don't think so. But what he did do was tie Heather up in his bedroom closet, standing up and wearing his high school jacket—and nothing else—and force her to suck on Popsicles all night."

"How did he force her?"

"He would tickle her if she stopped. Heather was very ticklish. She worked those Popsicles until the sun came up. Said when she got home she felt as if she had gargled a whole pint of novocaine."

"But he didn't hurt her in any way?"

"Her wrists had rope burns on them, but other than that she was fine. I tried to get her to talk to the police about what had happened, but she wouldn't. She wanted to go out with him again! I said no way. I went to Eddie and told him if he saw Heather again, I would personally speak to the police about his collection of snuff films. They're illegal, you know. Of course you know that! You work for the FBI. Sorry, I forgot that for a moment, with you just sitting there looking so young and everything. Anyway, Eddie backed off 'cause he didn't want to lose his job. Jesus, I tell you, that guy was born to work with the dead. You'd think they were his Barbie dolls."

"You said he loved the corpse that was stolen. What do you mean?"

"He was always fooling with it."

"Exactly how did he fool with it?"

"I don't know. He just always had it out is all."

"Didn't anyone tell him to stop fooling with it?"

Sally giggled. "No! The corpse never complained."

I pause a moment to take this all in. Fooling with Yaksha's remains might mean fooling with his blood. Could the blood of a dead vampire make a living vampire? I didn't know.

"He didn't bother Heather again?" I ask.

"No."

"Did he take any revenge on you for threatening him?"

Sally hesitated; her natural gaiety faltered. "I don't know for sure. I had an old cat, Sibyl, that I'd owned since she was born. I was very fond of her. Two days after I spoke to Eddie, I found her dead in my backyard."

"How did she die?"

"Don't know. There wasn't a mark on her. I didn't

bring her to a vet for an autopsy." Sally shivered. "I get enough of that here. You understand."

"I do. I'm sorry about your cat. Tell me—did Eddie have startling green eyes, bony hands, and an acne-scarred face?"

Sally nods. "That's him. Has he killed anybody?"

I stand. I feel no relief that I have found my man. He is worse than I feared.

"Yes," I say. "He is making his own snuff films now."

5 ～⌒

We are the only ones sitting at the end of Water Cove
Pier, where Slim and his people came for me with
their many guns and unbreakable handcuffs. It is too
cold for most people to eat outside, but we are
bundled up. We eat fish and chips and feed the birds.
The sun is bright and reflects off the calm water, and
the chilly air is heavy with the smell of salt. I wear
dark sunglasses and a hat. I like hats, red and black
ones.

The first time I ever saw the sea I was already a
vampire. So I don't know what it looks like to a
mortal. The many fish, the seaweed, and the shells—I
see them even in murky water. For me the ocean is a
huge aquarium, teeming with visible life, food. In

moments of extreme thirst I have drunk the blood of fish, of sharks even. Once, in the seventeenth century, off the coast of what is now Big Sur, I even killed a great white shark, but not for food. The thing tried to bite off my legs.

I think of Yaksha without his legs.

And I ask myself the impossible question.

Could he still be alive?

Joel holds in his hand the papers he obtained from the coroner, the details on Edward Fender—Eddie. I will relieve him of the papers in a few minutes. But first I want to talk to him because I want to keep him from talking. Honestly, I do not want to kill him. He is a good man—I see that. More interested in helping humanity than in being applauded. But to convince him to keep his mouth shut, I have to tell him even more about the enemy, and myself. And then I will have even more reason to kill him. It is a paradox. Life is that way. God designed it that way. I believe I met him once. He was full of mischief.

I will say things I never should say to any mortal. Because I am hurt, I feel my own mortality. The feeling gives me reason to be reckless.

"Do you often come here?" Joel asks, referring to Water Cove, which is twenty miles south of Mayfair. "Or go down to Seaside?"

"No." My weakness haunts me like a second shadow. If I do not drink soon, and a lot, I will be in no shape to return to Los Angeles tonight. "Why do you ask?"

"I was just thinking how you told me your house

exploded six weeks ago. By strange coincidence there was a group of violent murders in Seaside at that same time. I believe they occurred a day before you said you lost your house, if my memory serves me correctly."

"You have a good memory."

He waits for me to elaborate, but I don't. "Were you and your friend connected with those murders as well?" he asks.

I peer at him through my dark lenses. "Why do you ask?"

"One of the people killed at a gas station in Seaside was a woman. Her skull was cracked open by an exceptionally strong person. The coroner told me about it. He said it would take a monster to do what had been done to her." He pauses, adds, "The manner of her death reminds me of what's happening in Los Angeles."

I offer a bird one of my french fries. Animals generally like me, if I'm not chasing them. "Do you think I'm a monster, Joel?"

"You cannot keep answering my questions with questions."

"But one answer always leads to another question." I shrug. "I'm not interested in discussing my life story with you."

"Were you there that night those people died in Seaside?"

I pause. "Yes."

He sucks in a breath. "Did your friend kill that woman?"

A white dove takes my fry. I wipe off my hands on

my skirt. "No. My friend sent that woman to kill me."

"Some friend."

"He had his reasons."

Joel sighs. "I'm getting nowhere with you. Just tell me what you're trying to tell me and be done with it."

"Eddie Fender is our man."

"You don't know that."

"I do. To me, it's a fact. And the other thing is—I like you and I don't want you to get hurt. You have to leave Eddie to me."

He snorts. "Right. Thank you, Alisa, but I can take care of myself."

I touch his arm, hold his eyes, even through my dark glasses. "You don't understand what you're up against. You don't understand me." I let the tips of my fingers slide over the sleeve of his jacket. I hold his hand. Despite my weakness, his proximity is stimulating. Even without trying, my gaze weakens him. Better to kiss him, I think, than to kill him. But then I think of Ray, whom I love. He will be waking soon. The sun nears the horizon. The orange glow lights Joel's face as if he were sitting in a desolate purgatory, where the judgment of the damned and the saved had already been completed, five thousand years ago. He sits so close to me, but I cannot welcome him too far into my world without devouring his, as I did Ray's. But I do have to scare him, yes, and deeply. I add, "I was the one who killed that woman."

He smiles nervously. "Sure. How did you do it? With your bare hands?"

I take his hand. "Yes."

"You must be very strong?"

"Yes."

"Alisa."

"Sita. My name is Sita."

"Why do you go by Alisa?"

I shrug. "It's a name. Only those I care about call me Sita."

"What do you want me to call you?"

I smile sadly. "What would you prefer to call a murderer?"

He takes his hand from mine and stares at the ocean a moment. "Sometimes when I talk to you I feel like I'm talking to a mental case. Only you're too together to be labeled unstable."

"Thank you."

"You weren't serious about having killed that woman, were you?"

I speak in a flat voice. "It happened at the corner of Fryer and Tads. The woman was found on the floor of the women's room. Her brains were on the floor as well. Like you said, her head had been cracked open, the front of it. That was because I grabbed her from behind when I rammed her face into the wall." I sip my Coke. "Did the coroner give you these details?"

I see from Joel's stunned face that the coroner must have enlightened him on some of the facts. He can't quit staring at me. For him, I know, it is as if my eyes are as big as the sea, as black as the deepest subterranean crevasse. Beneath the ocean is molten bedrock.

Beneath my eyes I believe he senses an ageless fire. Yet he shivers and I understand why. My words are so cold.

"It's true," he whispers.

"Yes. I am not normal." Standing, I pluck the papers from his hand before he can blink. My eyes bore down on him. "Go home, Joel, to wherever home is. Don't try to follow me. Don't talk about me. If you do, I will know about it and I will have to come after you. You don't want that, any more than you want to take on this murderer. He is like me, and at the same time he is not like me. We are both cruel, but his cruelty is without reason, without kindness. Yes, I did kill that woman, but I didn't do so out of malice. I can be very kind, when it suits me. But when I am cornered, I am as dangerous as this Eddie. I have to corner him, you see, in a special place, under special circumstances. It's the only way to stop him. But you can't be there. If you are, you will die. You will die anyway, if you don't leave me alone. Do you understand?"

He stares at me as if I am a distorted apparition trying to materialize from a realm he never knew existed. "No," he mumbles.

I take a step back. "Try to arrest me."

"Huh?"

"Arrest me. I have admitted to killing a woman with my bare hands. I know details of the crime only the killer could know. It's your responsibility as an FBI agent to bring me in. Take out your gun and read me my rights. Now!"

My pounding gaze has short-circuited his brain synapses. But he does stand, and he does pull out his gun and point it at me. "You're under arrest," he says.

I slap the gun away. It lands a hundred yards off in the water. But for him it is just gone. His stunned expression, even in the ruby light, goes pale.

"You see," I say softly. "You can't play this game with me. You don't have the proper equipment. Your gun is on the bottom of the sea. Believe me, Joel, trust me—or you will end up in the bottom of a grave." I pat his shoulder as I step past him. "There will be a bus along soon. There is a stop at the entrance to the pier. Goodbye."

6 ~~

Ray should *not* come with me to Los Angeles. I feel this in my heart. But after the sun sets, and he awakens, and I explain to him what is happening in L.A., he insists on joining me. How he shudders at the thought of more vampires! How his horror breaks my heart, even though intellectually I share his opinion. Truly, he still sees us as evil. But, he says, two are stronger than one, and I know his math makes sense. I might very well need him at a critical moment. Also, unless I take him with me, I know he will go another night without feeding. How many nights he can survive, I don't know. I can endure for as long as six months without drinking blood. As long as I don't have other vampires throwing knives in me, that is.

Anxious to get down to Los Angeles, we fly south in my Learjet without feeding. But once on the ground, before we do anything else, I tell Ray we are going hunting. He agrees reluctantly, and I have to promise him we will not hurt anybody. It is a promise I make reluctantly. Opening large veins, I never know what complications might result.

We go to Zuma Beach, north of Malibu. The beaches have always been a favorite den of victims for me. Plenty of out-of-state travelers, homeless people, drunks—portions of the population who are not immediately missed. Of course, I seldom kill my meal tickets these day, since I have begun to believe in miracles, or since I have fallen in love with my reluctant Count Dracula, whichever came first. Actually, I once met Vlad the Impaler, the real man Count Dracula was based on, in the fifteenth century in Transylvania during the war with the Ottoman Turks. Forget those stories about his mean-looking canines. Now, there was a fellow who needed modern dentistry. His teeth were rotting out of his mouth, and he had the worst breath. He was no vampire, just a Catholic zealot with a fetish for decapitation. He asked me out, though, for a ride in his carriage. I attract unusual men. I told him where to stuff it. I believe I invented the phrase.

Driving north on the Coast Highway, I spot a young couple on the beach making out on their sleeping bags. Up and down the beach, for at least half a mile, there isn't another soul. Looks like dinner to me, but Ray has his doubts. He always does. I swear, if we were a normal couple going out to a restaurant, he would never be satisfied with the menu. Being a vampire, you can't be a picky eater, it just doesn't work. Yet you might wonder—what about blood-borne diseases? What about AIDS? None of them matters. None of them can touch us. Our blood is a fermented black soup—it strips to the bone whatever we sink our teeth into. This particular young couple looks healthy and happy to me, a blood type I prefer. It is true I am sensitive to the "life vibration" of those I feed upon. Once I drank the blood of a well-known rap singer and had a headache for a week.

"What is wrong with them?" I ask Ray as we park a hundred yards north of them. They are behind and below us, not far from the reach of the surf. The waves are big, the tide high.

"They're not much older than I am," he says.

"Yes? Would it be better if they were both in their eighties?"

"You don't understand."

"I do understand. They remind you of the life you left behind. But I need blood. I shouldn't have to explain that to you. I suffered two serious wounds last night, and then I had to feed you when I returned home."

"I didn't ask you to feed me."

I throw up my hands. "And I didn't ask to have to watch you die. Please, Ray, let's do this quick so that we can take care of what we came for."

"How are we going to approach them?"

I open my car door. "There's going to be no

approach. We are simply going to rush them and grab them and start drinking their blood."

Ray grabs my arm. "No. They'll be terrified. They'll run to the police."

"The police in this town have more important matters to deal with than a couple of hysterical twenty-year-olds."

Ray is stubborn. "It will take you only a few moments to put them at ease and hypnotize them. Then they won't suffer."

I stand up outside the car and scowl at him. "You would rather I suffer."

Ray wearily climbs out of his side of the car. "No, Sita. I would prefer to fast."

I walk around and take his hand—a handsome young couple out for an innocent stroll. But my mood is foul. "You would rather I suffer," I repeat.

The blond couple doesn't even look up as we approach, so entranced are they in each other's anatomy. I throw Ray another unpleasant glance. I am supposed to hypnotize these two? He shrugs—he would prefer I anesthetize them before pinching their veins. My patience has reached its limit. Striding over to the hot-blooded boy and girl, I reach down and grab their sleeping bag and pull it out from under them. They fly three feet in the air—literally. They look up at me as if I might bite them. Imagine.

"You are about to be mugged," I say. "It will be a novelty mugging. You will not be hurt and you will not lose any money. But you are going to perform us a great service. Stay calm and we'll be done in ten minutes."

They do *not* remain calm. I don't care. I grab the girl and throw her to Ray, and then I am on the guy. Pulling his arms behind his back and pinning them there with one hand, I don't worry when he opens his mouth and screams for help. With the pounding surf, no one will hear him. Not that it would make much difference if someone did. In L.A. the earth could shake and people would think it was the Harmonic Convergence. A little screaming on Zuma Beach never worried anyone. Yet I do end up clamping the guy's mouth shut with my free hand.

"I prefer to dine in silence," I say. Glancing over at Ray who is struggling with the girl—for no reason—I remark in his direction, "You make it worse by dragging it out."

"I do things my own way," he says.

"Hmm," I grunt. Closing my eyes, using my long thumbnail to open a neck vein, I press my lips on the torn flesh and suck hard. I have cut the carotid artery. The blood gushes into my mouth like hot chocolate poured over ice cream. My young man goes limp in my arms and begins to enjoy the sensation. For me and my victim, feeding can be intensely sensual. I know he feels as if every nerve in his body is being caressed by a thousand fingers. And for me the blood is a warm pulsing river. But if I wish, feeding can be terrifying for my victim. By the time I finished with Slim, for example, he felt as if hell would be a welcome respite.

None of my victims, of course, becomes a vampire simply by being bitten. There has to be a massive exchange of blood to bring about that transformation. I wonder if Eddie Fender has needles and syringes.

So caught up am I in replenishing my strength that I don't immediately notice that we are three when we should be four. Opening my eyes, I see that Ray's girl has escaped. She is running down the beach at high speed, soundlessly, in the direction of concrete steps that will lead her past the beach boulders and back up onto the Coast Highway.

"What the hell!" I say to Ray.

He shrugs. "She bit my hand."

"Go get her. No, I'll get her." I hand over my happy boy. "Finish with this guy. He's good for another pint."

Ray accepts the young man reluctantly. "His strength is ebbing."

"You worry about your own strength," I call over my shoulder as I chase after the girl. She's a hundred yards away, on the verge of leaping onto the steps—it is a wonder that she hasn't started screaming yet. I have to assume she is in shock. She is ten feet from the highway when I pounce on her and drag her back down the steps. There is more fight in her than I expect, however. Whirling, she punches me hard in the chest. To my great surprise, the blow hurts. She has hit me exactly where the stake penetrated my heart. But my grip on her does not falter. "This is going to hurt, sister," I tell her as she stares at me in horror.

My right hand pins her arms, my left closes her mouth. Again, the thumbnail opens her big neck vein. But I am even more eager than before and suck her red stream as if I am drinking from the elixir of immortality itself, as indeed I am. Yet it is not the matter, the fluids or elements in the blood, that grant the vampire his or her longevity. It is the *life*—that essence that no scientist has ever been able to replicate in his laboratory—that makes any other source of nourishment pale by comparison. But this feeding with this girl is not erotic—it is ravenous. Feeling as if I am trying to drown my pain and weariness in one gulp, I drink from this girl as if her life is my reward for all the evildoers I have been forced to bring to justice.

Yet my thirst deludes even my sense of right and wrong. My vast experience fails me. Suddenly I feel Ray shaking me, telling me to let go. Opening my eyes, I notice the boy lying lazily on the beach, still a hundred yards away, sleeping off his unexpected encounter with the creatures of the night. He will wake with a bad headache, nothing more. The girl in my arms is another matter. Desperately pale, cold as the sand we stand on, she wheezes. Her heart flutters inside her chest. Crouching down, I lay her on her back on the beach. Ray kneels across from me and shakes his head. My guilt is a bitter-tasting dessert.

"I didn't mean to do this," I say. "I got carried away."

"Is she going to make it?" Ray asks.

Placing my hand over her chest, I take a pulse

reading that tells me more than an intensive care unit filled with modern equipment could. It is only then that I note the girl's heart is scarred—the right aorta; possibly from a childhood disease. It is not as though I have drained her completely. Yet I have taken more from her than I should have, and in combination with her anatomical weakness, I know she is not going to make it.

"It doesn't look good," I say.

Ray takes her hand. He has not reached for my hand in over a month. "Can't you do something for her?" he asks, pain in his voice.

I spread my hands. "What can I do? I cannot put the blood I have taken back inside her. It's done—let's get out of here."

"No! We can't just leave her. Use your power. Save her. You saved me."

I briefly close my eyes. "I saved you by changing you. I cannot change her."

"But she'll die."

I stare at him across my handiwork. "Yes. Everyone who is born dies."

He refuses to accept the situation. "We have to get her to a hospital." He goes to lift her. "They can give her a transfusion. She might make it."

I stop him, gently, slowly removing his hands from the girl's body. Folding her hands across her chest, I listen as her heart begins to skip inside. Yet I continue to look at my lover, searching his expression for signs of hatred or the realization that this being he is to spend the rest of eternity with is really a witch. But Ray only looks grieved, and somehow that makes it worse for me.

"She is not going to live," I say. "She would never make it to a hospital. Her heart is weak. I failed to notice that at the start. I was so thirsty—I got carried away. It happens sometimes. I am not perfect. This is not a perfect creation. But if it is any consolation, I am sorry that this has happened. If I could heal her, I would. But Krishna did not give me that ability." I add, "I can only kill."

Ray follows the girl's breathing for a minute. That is all the time it lasts. The girl gives a soft strangled sound and her back arches off the sandy floor. Then she lies still. Standing, I silently take Ray by the hand and lead him back to the car. Long ago I learned that death cannot be discussed. It is like talking about darkness. Both topics bring only confusion—especially to us, who have to go on living through the night. All who are born die, I think, remembering Krishna's words. All who die will be reborn. In his profound wisdom he spoke the words to comfort all those born in Kali Yuga, the age in which we now live, the dark age. Yet it's strange, as we get in the car and drive away from the beach, I cannot remember his eyes, exactly what they looked like. The sky is covered with haze. The stars, the moon—they are not out. I cannot think what it means to be young. All is indeed dark.

7

When I met Private Investigator Michael Riley, Ray's father, he talked to me about my previous residence. Trying to impress me with how much he knew about my wealth.

"Prior to moving to Mayfair, you lived in Los Angeles—in Beverly Hills, in fact—at Two-Five-Six Grove Street. Your home was a four-thousand-square-foot mansion, with two swimming pools, a tennis court, a sauna, and a small observatory. The property is valued at six-point-five million. To this day you are listed as the sole owner, Miss Perne."

I was very impressed with Riley's knowledge. That was one of the main reasons I killed him. It is to this house we go after Zuma Beach. Mr. Riley forgot to mention the mansion's deep basement. It is here I keep a stockpile of sophisticated weapons: Uzis, grenade launchers, high-powered laser-assisted sniper rifles, 10-millimeter pistols equipped with silencers— toys easily purchased on any Middle Eastern black market. Loading up my car, I feel like Rambo, who must have been a vampire in a previous incarnation. Loved the way that guy snapped people's necks. Ray watches me pile on the weapons with a bewildered expression.

"You know," he says, "I've never even fired a gun."

That concerns me. Just because he's a vampire he's not necessarily a crack shot, although he could quickly become one with a couple of lessons. Myself, I have practiced with every weapon I own. My skill is such that I use every gun to its full capacity.

"Just don't shoot yourself in the foot," I say.

"I thought you were going to say, just don't shoot me."

"That, too," I say, feeling uneasy.

Edward Fender's job application and résumé contain only one permanent address, which is his mother's. It is my belief that the lead is valid. Mrs. Fender's house is located only four miles west of the Coliseum, in the city of Inglewood, a suburb of Los Angeles. It is a quarter after nine by the time we park in front of her place. Rolling down the window and bidding Ray to sit silently, I listen carefully to what's going on inside the residence. The TV is on to "Wheel of Fortune."

An elderly woman sits in a rocking chair reading a magazine. Her lungs are weak; she has a slight dry cough. A front window of the house is half open. The interior is dusty and damp. It smells of poor health and of human serpents. A vampire has recently been in the house, but he is no longer there. Now I am absolutely certain of the identity of the monster I pursue.

"He was here less than two hours ago," I whisper to Ray.

"Is he in the area?"

"No. But he can come into the area swiftly. He has at least twice my speed. I am going to speak to the woman alone. I want you to park out of sight down the street. If you see someone approach the house, don't try to warn me. Drive off. I will know he is coming. I will deal with him. Do you understand?"

Ray is amused. "Am I in the army? Do I have to take your orders?"

I take his hand. "Seriously, Ray. In a situation like this you can't help me. You can only hurt me." I let go of him and slip a small revolver into my coat pocket. "I just have to put a couple of bullets in his brain, and he will not be making any more vampires. Then we can go after the others. They will be a piece of cake."

"Do you like cake, Sita?"

I have to smile. "Yes, of course. With ice cream, especially."

"You never told me when your birthday is. Do you know?"

"Yes." I lean over and kiss him. "It is the day I met you. I was reborn on that day."

He kisses me back, grabs my arm as I go to leave. "I don't blame you, you know."

I nod, although I don't completely believe him. "I know."

The woman answers the door a moment after I knock and remains behind the torn screen door. Her hair is white, her face in ruins. Her hands are arthritic; the fingers claw at the air like hungry rats' paws. She has flat gray eyes that look as if they have watched black-and-white television for decades. There is little feeling in them, except perhaps a sense of cynical contempt. Her bathrobe is a tattered gown of food and bloodstains. Some of the latter look fresh. There are red marks on her neck, still healing.

Her son has been drinking her blood.

I smile quickly. "Hello. Mrs. Fender? I'm Kathy Gibson, a friend of your son's. Is he at home?"

My beauty, my smooth bearing throw her off balance. I shudder to think of the women Eddie usually brings home to Mother. "No. He works the graveyard shift. He won't be home till late." She pauses, gives me a critical examination. "What did you say your name is?"

"Kathy." My voice goes sweet and soft, strangely persuasive. "I didn't mean to stop by so late. I hope I'm not disturbing you?"

She shrugs. "Just watching TV. How come I've never heard Eddie mention you before?"

I stare at her. "We only just met a few days ago. My brother introduced us." I add, "He works with Eddie."

"At the clinic?"

The woman is trying to trick me. I frown. "Eddie doesn't work at a clinic."

The woman relaxes slightly. "At the warehouse?"

"Yes. At the warehouse." My smile broadens. My gaze penetrates deeper. This woman is mentally unstable. She has secret perversions. My eyes do not cause her to flinch. She is fond of young women, I know, little girls even. I wonder about Mr. Fender. I add, "May I come in?"

"Pardon?"

"I have to make a call. May I use your phone?" I add, "Don't worry, I don't bite."

I have pushed the right button. She enjoys being bitten. Her son drinks her blood with her consent. Even I, an immoral beast, have never been drawn to incestuous relationships. Of course, in the literal sense of the word, we are not talking about incest. Still, the Brady Bunch would never survive in this house. She opens the screen door for me.

"Of course," she says. "Please come in. Who do you have to call?"

"My brother."

"Oh."

I step inside, my sense of smell on alert. Eddie has recently slept in this house. She must let him sleep away the days, not questioning his aversion to the sun. My ability to handle the sun is hopefully my ace in the hole against this creature. Even Yaksha, many times more powerful than myself, was far less comfortable in the sun than I am. Secretly I pray Eddie can't even leave the house in the daylight hours without wearing sunscreen with an SPF of 100 or better, like Ray. Although my senses study the interior of the house, my ears never leave the exterior. I cannot be taken unaware, like before. Mrs. Fender leads me to the phone beside her rocking chair. Her reading material lies partially hidden beneath a dirty dishrag—a back issue of *Mad Magazine*. Actually, I kind of like *Mad Magazine*.

I dial a phony number and speak to no one. I'm at Eddie's house. He's not here. I'll be a few minutes late. Goodbye. Setting down the phone, I stare at the woman again.

"Has Eddie called here tonight?" I ask.

"No. Why would he call? He just left a couple of hours ago."

I take a step toward her. "No one's called?"

"No."

She's lying. The FBI has called, probably Joel himself. Yet Joel, or anyone else for that matter—with the exception of Eddie—has not been in the house recently. I would smell their visit. Yet that situation will soon change. The authorities will converge on this place sooner or later. That fact may not be as crucial as it appears. Eddie would not easily walk into a trap, and clearly he does not meet with his cohorts in this house. The warehouse is the key. I need the address. Taking another step forward, I force the woman to back against a divider that separates the meager living room from the messy kitchen. My eyes are all over her, all she sees. There is no time for subtlety. Fear blossoms inside her chest but also awe. Her will is weird but weak. I stop only a foot away.

"I am going to visit Eddie now," I say softly. "Tell me the best way to the warehouse from here."

She speaks like a puppet. "Take Hawthorne Boulevard east to Washington. Turn right and go down to Winston." She blinks and coughs. "It's there."

I press my face to her face. She breathes my air, my intoxicating scent. "You will not remember that I was here. There is no Kathy Gibson. There is no pretty blond girl. No visitor stopped by. The FBI didn't even call. But if they should call again, tell them you haven't heard from your son in a long time." I put my palm on the woman's forehead, whisper in her ear. "You understand?"

She stares into space. "Yes."

"Good." My lips brush her neck, but I don't bite. But if Eddie pisses me off again, I swear, I am going to strangle his mother in front of him. "Goodbye, Mrs. Fender."

Yet as I leave the house I note a cold draft from the back rooms. I feel the vibration of an electric motor and smell coolant. The house has a large freezer next to one of the back bedrooms. I almost turn to explore more. I have planted my suggestions, however, and to return may upset the woman's delicate state of illusion. Also, I have the location of the warehouse, and finding Eddie is my first priority. If need be, I can return later and search the rest of the house.

8 ～～～

"Tell me about your husband Rama?" Ray asks as we drive toward the warehouse. "And your daughter, Lalita?"

The question takes me by surprise. "It was a long time ago."

"But you remember everything?"

"Yes." I sit silently for a moment. "I was almost twenty when we met. Three or four times a year merchants used to pass by that portion of India that is now known as Rajastan. We lived between the desert and the jungle. The merchants would sell us hats to keep off the sun, herb potions to drive away the bugs. Rama was the son of a merchant. I first saw him by the river that flowed beside our village. He was teaching a small child how to fly a kite. We had kites in those days. We invented them, not the Chinese." I shake my head. "When I saw him, I just knew."

Ray understands but asks anyway, anxious to dwell on my humanity in the light of what happened at the beach. "What did you know?"

"That I loved him. That we belonged together." I smile at the memory. "He was named after an earlier incarnation of Lord Vishnu—the eighth avatar, or incarnation of God. Lord Rama was married to the Goddess Sita. Krishna was supposed to be the ninth avatar. I worshipped Lord Vishnu from the time I was born. Maybe that's why I got to meet Krishna. Anyway, you can see how Rama's and my names went together. Maybe our union was destined to be. Rama was like you in a lot of ways. Quiet, given to thoughtful pauses." I glance over. "He even had your eyes."

"They were the same?"

"They did not look the same. But they were the same. You understand?"

"Yes. Tell me about Lalita?"

"Lalita is one of the names of the Goddess as well. It means 'She who plays.' She was up to mischief the moment she came out of my womb. Ten months old and she would climb out of her cradle and crawl and walk all the way to the river." I chuckle. "I remember once I found her sitting with a snake in one of the small boats our people had. Fortunately the snake was asleep. It was poisonous! I remember how frightened I was." I sigh. "You wouldn't have known me in those days."

"I wish I had known you then."

His remark is sweet—he means it that way—yet it stings. My hands fidget on the steering wheel. "I wish many things," I whisper.

"Do you believe in reincarnation?" he asks suddenly.

"Why do you ask?"

"Just curious. Do you?"

I consider. "I know Krishna said it was a reality. Looking back, I believe he always spoke the truth. But I never talked to him about it. I scarcely talked to him at all."

"If reincarnation is a reality, then what about us? Are we evolving toward God? Or are we stuck because we're afraid to die?"

"I have asked myself the same questions, many times. But I've never been able to answer them."

"Can't you at least answer one of them?"

"Which one is that?" I ask.

"Are you afraid?"

I reach over and take his hand. "I don't fear death for myself."

"But to fear it at all—isn't it the same difference? If you trust Krishna, then you must trust that there is no death."

I force a smile. "We're a philosopher tonight."

He smiles. "Don't be anxious. I'm not thinking of suicide. I just think we have to look at the bigger picture."

I squeeze his hand and let go. "I believe Krishna saw all of life as nothing more than a motion picture projected onto a vast screen. Certainly nothing in this world daunted him. Even when I held his companion, Radha, in my clutches, he never lost his serenity."

Ray nods. "I would like to have such peace of mind."

"Yes. So would I."

His reaches over and touches my long hair. "Do you think I am Rama?"

I have to take a breath. My eyes moisten. My words come out weak. "I don't understand."

"Yes, you do. Did I come back for you?"

There are tears on my face. They are five thousand years old. I remember them. After Yaksha changed me, I saw neither my husband nor my daughter again. How I hated him for doing that to me. Yet, had I never become a vampire, I never would have met Ray. But I shake my head at his questions.

"I don't know," I say.

"Sita—"

"When I met you," I interrupt, "I felt as if Krishna had led me to you." I reach up and press his hand to the side of my face. "You feel like Rama. You smell like him."

He leans over and kisses my ear. "You're great."

"You're wonderful."

He brushes away my tears. "They always paint Krishna as blue. I know you explained that it's symbolic. That he is blue like the vast sky—unbounded. But I dream about him sometimes, when you lie beside me. And when I do, his eyes are always blue, like shining stars." He pauses. "Have you ever had such a dream?"

I nod.

"Tell me about it?"

"Maybe later."

"All right. But didn't your husband die before he could have met Krishna?"

"Yes."

"So I can't be remembering a past life?"

"I don't know. I wouldn't think so."

Ray lets go of me and sits back, seemingly disappointed. He adds casually, "I never dream of blood. Do you?"

Often, I think. Maybe once, five thousand years ago, we had more in common. Yet I lie to him, even though I hate to lie to those I love. Even though I have promised myself and him that I would stop.

"No," I say. "Never."

We park two blocks away from the warehouse, a gray rectangular structure as long as a football field, as tall as a lighthouse. But no light emanates from this building. The exterior walls are rotting wood, moldy plaster, panes of glass so drenched in dust they could be squares etched on the walls of a coal mine. The surrounding fence is tall, barbed—a good stretch of wire on which to hang fresh corpses. Yet the occupants are more subtle than that, but not a lot more. Even from this distance I smell the decaying bodies they have ravaged inside, and I know the police and the

FBI are seriously underestimating Los Angeles's recent violent crime wave. The odor of the yakshini, the snakes from beyond the black vault of the universe, also wafts from the building. I estimate a dozen vampires inside. But is Eddie one of them? And how many of his partners presently walk the streets? Vicious dogs wander the perimeter. They look well fed.

"Do you have a plan?" Ray asks.

"Always."

"I want to be part of it."

I nod. "You realize the danger."

"I just have to look in the mirror, sister."

I smile. "We have to burn this building down with all of them inside. To do that we need large quantities of gasoline, and the only way we are going to get that is to steal a couple of gasoline trucks from a nearby refinery."

"With our good looks and biting wit, that shouldn't be too hard."

"Indeed. The hard part will come when we try to plant our trucks at either end of the building and ignite them. First we'll have to cut the fence, so we can drive in unobstructed, and to do that we will have to silently kill all the dogs. But I think I can take them out from this distance using a silencer on one of my rifles."

Ray winces. "Is that necessary?"

"Yes. Better a few dead dogs than the end of humanity. The main thing is, we must attack *after* dawn, when they're all back inside and feeling sleepy. That includes our prize policymaker—Eddie."

"I like to take a nap at that time myself," Ray remarks.

I speak seriously. "You are going to have to be strong with the sun in the sky, and drive one of the trucks. I know that won't be easy for you. But if all goes well, you can seek shelter immediately afterward."

He nods. "Sounds like a piece of cake."

"No. It's a baked Alaska." I study the structure and nod. "They'll burn."

Yet my confidence is a costume. The previous night, when I stared into Eddie's eyes, he seemed insane, but also shrewd. The ease with which we have found him and his people disturbs me. The stage is set for a snuff film, big time. But I have to wonder who is directing the show. Whether it will go straight onto the front pages of the *Los Angeles Times*. Or end up buried in video, in Eddie's private collection.

We crouch in the shadows two blocks down the street from the warehouse as I load my high-powered rifle, especially equipped with laser-guided scope and fat silencer. At our backs are two gasoline trucks, with two huge tankers hooked on to each one. We didn't even have to go to a refinery to steal them. Leaving the ghetto, we just spotted the blasted things heading toward the freeway. I *accidentally* pulled in front of one and got my car slightly damaged. Both drivers climbed out, and I started screaming at them. How dare you ruin my brand-new car! I just bought it! Man, you are going to pay big time!

Then I smacked their heads together and took their keys. I figure they should be waking up soon, in the

Dumpster where I dropped them. Ray helped me drive one of the tankers back to the warehouse. For once, he seemed to be enjoying himself—the thrill of the hunt. Then the sun came up. Since that time, fifteen minutes ago, he has been hiding under a blanket and wiping at his burning eyes. He doesn't complain, though. He never does.

I finish loading the rifle and prop my left elbow on one knee, steadying the barrel in the direction of the big black dog closest to our end of the lot. Not only do I have to shoot each animal cleanly in the head, I must shoot between the holes in the wire fence. A stray bullet could ruin the whole plan. The dog growls as if sensing my attention, and I notice the blood that trickles from its saliva and the way it shakes when the sun catches in its eyes. Another Eddie Fender surprise.

An hour before dawn Eddie returned with a dozen partners. All together there are twenty-one vampires inside, all powerfully built males. With them they have two terrified Caucasian couples—breakfast. The four people started screaming the moment they were taken inside and didn't stop until their throats were ripped open. Ray paced miserably the whole time, insisting that we attack right then.

But I refused to risk the human race for the lives of four people.

"I would almost rather you were shooting people," Ray mumbles, hiding beneath the dirty orange covering. His blanket is a gift from a local homeless person. I gave the guy five hundred dollars for it and told him to flee the area. Although we are well shaded by a nearby brick wall, Ray's brow is covered by a film of sweat and he can't stop blinking. His bloodshot eyes look as if they have been sprayed with kerosene.

"If it's any consolation," I say, "these dogs are worse than rabid."

"What do you mean?"

"He has given them his blood."

"No way. Vampire dogs?"

"It could be worse. It could be vampire fish. Think of a school of those swimming the ocean. We'd never be able to find them all."

Ray chuckles weakly. "Can we go fishing up north after this is all over?"

"Sure. We can go salmon fishing in the streams in Washington. And you'll be pleased to know you won't need a fishing rod to catch them."

"I might still use a rod." He adds, "I used to go fishing with my dad."

"I did the same with my father," I say truthfully. Before Yaksha killed my father. Yaksha—where can his body be? And what shape is it in? Doubt continues to plague me, but I push it aside. Fixing my aim on the first dog, I whisper to Ray, "I'm going to do them quickly. Don't speak to me for a moment."

"Fine."

I peer into the dog's cruel eye through my scope. Pressing the trigger, there is a gentle *swish* of air. My caliber is small; nevertheless, the top of the dog's head comes off. Silently it topples over. Its partners hardly notice. But they will soon enough. They will smell the blood, and being infected with Eddie's blood, they may go crazy. But I don't give them the chance. Scarcely pausing between shots, I move from one beast to the next, killing all nine in less than a minute. I set the rifle down and pick up my wire cutters.

"Stay here until I return," I say. "Then be ready to move. If all goes according to plan, we'll be out of here in ten minutes."

Barefoot, soundlessly, I scurry toward the tall fence. Fortune continues to favor us. The hour is early and the street remains deserted. We are not all that far from the Coliseum, perhaps two miles, in a rundown industrial section of town. Cutting a hole in the fence would be unnecessary if I just wanted to ram the warehouse with our trucks and take a flying leap to safety. I have vetoed this idea for two reasons. I worry that Ray, in his weakened condition, would end up getting killed. Also, I believe a more deft approach will ensure we get all the vampires. My sensitive nose has determined that the warehouse was previously used as storage for foam rubber, and that there are still a large number of polyurethane sheets inside. Polyurethane is extremely flammable. It is our intention to quietly park our trucks at either end of the building, light the ten-second fuses attached to the explosive caps I have brought from my L.A. home, and dash for safety. The occupants will be caught between two crushing waves of expanding flame. Behind the warehouse stands the tall brick wall of another abandoned building. The fire will smash against that wall and cut off any chance of a rear escape. And if by chance any of the vampires do manage to get out of the inferno, I will be waiting for them beyond the perimeter of the fence with my rifle. They will go down as easily as the dogs. It is a good plan and it should work.

Still, I worry.

Kneeling by the fence, I quickly begin to cut the wires, searching for guards, or a head appearing at one of the filthy windows, or any sign of movement inside. All is silent and calm. Eddie's newly made vampires are undoubtedly sensitive to the sun and probably can't stand guard after dawn. He may be overconfident of his powers—that is my real hope. My cutters click like sharp electronic pulses over a telephone line. Soon I am laying the wire down on the broken asphalt ground. In less than five minutes I have opened a hole large enough to drive our trucks through. I retreat to Ray and the tankers. Huddling under his blanket, he peers up at me with feverish eyes.

"Wish it were a cloudy day," he mutters.

I nod. "An eclipse would be even better." I offer him my hand. "Are you ready to rock?"

He gets up slowly, his blanket still wrapped around his head, and studies my handiwork from afar. "Are they all asleep?"

"They seem to be."

"Are you sure Eddie's still inside?"

"I saw him go in. I never saw him come out. But he

could have sneaked out the back way." I shrug. "We may never get this good a chance. We have to strike now and we have to strike hard."

He nods. "Agreed." He limps toward his truck, and I help him into the driver's seat. "You know, Sita, I don't have a license to drive this big a rig. What we're doing is against the law."

"There are human laws and there are God's laws. We may not be the most lovable creatures in creation, but we are doing the best we can."

He studies me seriously, his entire face now flushed red, soaked in sweat. "Is that true? Is there anything good we can give to the world?"

I hug him. "If we can stop these creatures, our being here will have been justified a thousand times over." I kiss him. "I'm sorry I let the girl die."

He wraps his arm around me. "It wasn't your fault."

"I'm sorry I killed your father."

"Sita." He holds me at arm's length. "You're five thousand years old. You have too much history. You have to learn to live in the present."

I smile, feeling like a foolish child. It is not a bad feeling. Despite all I have seen and done, he is the wise one. Reaching up, I brush his hair aside, out of his eyes, and then all at once I am kissing him again.

"You do remind me of Rama," I whisper in his ear. "So much so that you must be him. Promise me, Ray, and I will promise you. We will stay together—always."

He doesn't answer right away, and I pull back slightly to see what the matter is. He has dropped his blanket and is staring in the direction of the sun, although not directly, since we are still in the shade. But I would think the move would just hurt his eyes more.

"The sky is so blue," he says thoughtfully. "So vast." He turns back to me and chuckles softly. "We're like those vampire fish, lost in that ocean."

I frown. "Ray?"

"I was just thinking of Krishna." He squeezes my hands. "I promise our love will survive." He glances at the warehouse. "You want me to go to the south side?"

"Yes, to the left. Follow me in. Stay close. Drive up with your door slightly ajar. Don't let it bang. Kill the engine as you pass the gate and coast in. Park as close as you can to the building. Don't close your door when you get out. As soon as you can, light the fuse and run. I will hear it burning and light mine. If they try to escape, I will cut them down. We will meet here when it's over. Then we can go fishing." I pause, wanting to add something else, not knowing what it is. "Be careful, Ray."

"You, too, Sita." He touches his heart. "Love you."

I touch mine. The pain is back; it is hard to breathe. Maybe it is a sign from God.

"Love you," I say.

We cruise toward the warehouse, me first. The hole in the gate easily accommodates the tankers. The head of a dead dog flattens as the front wheel of the rig rolls over it. Turning off the engine, I allow my momentum to carry me toward the rear of the building. My maneuver is trickier than his, and for that reason I have chosen it. I have to swing around the side of the building rather than slide straight in. But there are few human devices I am not master of, and I have drunk the blood of so many long-distance truckers over the years that one could say the skill is deep in my veins. I complete the turn smoothly and park and climb out. My two tankers stand less than five feet from the wall of the building. Out the corner of my eye I notice an ice-cream truck parked down the block.

Still, all is calm, all is quiet. Even to my acute hearing.

Ray's truck, on the far side of the building, has also halted. I hear him climb out of his rig and walk toward the rear of the tanks where I have set the fuse. Yet I hear him stop in midstride, and I don't hear the fuse burning. I count my heartbeats and wait for him to complete his task.

But all is quiet. The fuse stays unlit.

My heart begins to pound.

My rifle over my shoulder, I walk toward the rear of my truck, moving in Ray's direction. Something is wrong, I fear. I cannot ignite my tankers without knowing what the problem is. Yet I cannot explode my gasoline from a distance—at least not easily. A bullet may or may not accomplish the feat. Yet I cannot check on Ray without leaving the fuel. It is a paradox

CHRISTOPHER PIKE

once again—my whole life is. After a moment to consider, I reach out and unscrew the cap at the bottom of the rear tanker. The gasoline gushes out. The warehouse rests on an incline, my end higher than Ray's. Stepping around the corner of the building, the volatile fuel follows me in a bubbling stream, soaking my bare feet. I fear the fumes will alert whoever is inside, yet feel I have no choice. The gasoline runs ahead of me, down toward the other truck. Our bombs will become one.

Now I see Ray's truck, but I do not see him, nor his feet standing behind one of the tankers. Moving slowly, my rifle at the ready, I let my hearing precede me. Inside the building the status remains. Twenty-one vampires sleeping peacefully, their bellies full, their dreams dripping red. There is someone behind the truck, however. Two people, maybe.

Two vampires, maybe.

Faintly I hear their breathing. One is calm and easy. The other gasping, struggling, perhaps against a hand clamped over his mouth. In an instant I know what has happened. Eddie was lying in wait for us. He has caught Ray and is holding him hostage on the passenger side of the rig, standing on the step that leads up into the cab. Eddie is waiting for me to come for Ray, to poke my head out. Then he will pounce. I have made the mistake I swore I would not make. I have underestimated an enemy.

It was all a setup. Eddie wanted to trap me.

Yet I do not panic. I don't have time and the day

98

may yet be saved. My hearing has grown more acute over the centuries. I suspect that, even though Eddie is stronger than I, his senses are not as keen. He may not be aware that I am aware of him. The element of surprise may still be mine.

Once again I consider quickly. I can come at him from the left or the right. Or I can come at him from above. The latter seems the most dangerous move, and therefore probably carries with it the greatest element of surprise. I favor it. But I will not simply leap onto the roof of the rig. I will fly right over it. Holding my rifle firmly in my hands, I take several long strides before the truck and then kick up vigorously, as long jumpers do. Floating over a respectable chunk of the lot, over the truck cabin, I turn in midair, bringing the muzzle to bear where I calculate Eddie will be. But I am moving fast, very fast, and when I reach the other side of the truck, near the end of my downward arc, they are not there.

Damn.

So startled am I by their disappearance that I almost lose my footing as I hit the ground. It takes me a moment to get my bearings. And in that time Eddie casually walks out from behind the front of the truck, standing behind Ray, using him as a shield, his bony hands wrapped around my lover's neck. Eddie's speed continues to amaze. In the short time I was in the air, he managed to move out of harm's way. Yet it is not only his superior reflexes that shock me, but his ability to anticipate my moves. He reads me like an open book. But is that so amazing? After all, we are both predators. He shakes Ray to let me know his grip is deadly. For his part Ray appears calm. He believes I will save him. I wish I shared his belief.

Eddie grins. "Hello, Sita. So we meet again."

Yaksha must be alive for him to know my name. Yet I cannot believe Yaksha would betray me to this monster, even though we had been mortal enemies. Keeping my gun level and circling slowly, I study Eddie's expression. He appears to be more sedate than the previous night, slightly weary. Absorbing six bullets must have taken something out of him. Yet his eyes remain chilling. I wonder about his mother, his upbringing, what it takes to create a man who watches snuff films for pleasure. I understand that he has always felt an outcast, and that he spent the majority of his lonely nights imagining what he would do if he had unlimited power. Then it just fell into his lap. Like a gift from God. There is a bit of the fanatic in his eyes. He believes he is on a holy mission and has elected himself the main deity. That disturbs me even more. A prophet is more dangerous than a criminal. At least a criminal's needs are simple. A prophet requires constant stimulation. The false ones, at least. Eddie has not killed Ray yet because he wants to play with us. This is all right, I decide. I know many games.

The sun bothers Eddie, but he can bear it. He squints.

"Hello, Eddie," I say pleasantly. "You look well."

"Thank you. You've made a nice recovery yourself. Congratulations on finding me so quickly. I thought it would take you at least a week to locate the warehouse." He adds, "How did you find me?"

His voice is a strange brew—crafty and eager, easy and sick. There is no depth to his tone, however, and I wonder if he is susceptible to my gentle words. Trying to shoot him while he holds Ray is out of the question. At any one instant he barely shows an inch of himself.

He knew I was in the area because he was waiting to ambush us. But his remarks show that he does not know I visited his mother, or how I probed his past.

"You leave a unique trail," I say softly. "I just had to follow the *red* brick road."

He is amused. And annoyed. He is a pile of contradictions, I see. He shakes Ray hard and my lover gasps. "Answer my question," he orders.

"What will you give me in return?" I continue to circle at a distance of thirty feet. So far there is no movement from inside the warehouse. I do not believe he has an accomplice who can help him. The gasoline from my draining tanker puddles nearby, although none of us is standing directly in it. Once again I try to plant my words in his mind. But the ground there is not fertile.

"I will let your boyfriend live," Eddie says.

"Why don't we do this? Let my friend go and I will answer all your questions. I will even set aside this shiny new gun."

"Set it aside first and I will consider your suggestion," Eddie replies.

My voice has yet to affect his mind. Still, I continue to try. "It is clear we don't trust each other. We can remain stalemated for a long time. Neither of us wants that. Let me offer you something in exchange for my friend's release. You're a newborn vampire. I am very old. There are many secrets to using your powers that I could teach you. Alone, it would take you several centuries to discover those secrets. To be what you want to be, you need me."

"But how do I know you will give me these secrets?" he asks. "How do I know that the moment I release your friend you won't open fire on me?"

"Because I need you," I lie, but persuasively. "Your blood is more powerful than my own. We can have an even exchange—your power for my knowledge."

Eddie considers. "Give me an example of one of your secrets."

"You have already seen an example. I am here today, right now. You do not know how I got here so quickly. A secret led me to you. I can give you that secret, and others, if you will release my friend."

"You have an interesting voice."

"Thank you."

Eddie's voice hardens. "Is that one of your secrets? The manner in which you manipulate people?"

His question stuns me. He misses nothing, and if that is the case he is not going to release Ray because he must know I will kill him. I consider a dangerous alternative.

"I manipulate mortals like puppets," I reply. "It is not so easy to manipulate *powerful* vampires. But weaker ones—like many of your followers—I could show you how to control them. You know, Eddie, the more you make, and the more they make, the less control you will have."

"I don't believe that."

"You will. Listen to me with an open mind. This is a rare opportunity for you. If you do not take it, you will regret it. You will also die. You're so young. You feel so powerful. But you have made a big mistake confronting me unarmed. This rifle can fire many bullets before having to be reloaded. Your body cannot withstand what I will do to you. If you kill my friend, I will kill you. It's that simple."

He is undaunted. "You may be old and full of secrets, but you have made the big mistake. This guy is important to you. I have his life in my hands. If you do not put down your rifle, I will kill him." His grip tightens and suddenly Ray is unable to breathe. "Put it down now."

"You dare to threaten me, punk." I raise my rifle and point it at Ray's chest. "Release him now."

Eddie remains determined. "Did they play poker thousands of years ago? I don't think so. You don't know how to bluff. Put it down, I say. Your friend is already turning blue."

"Blue is better than red," I reply. "But a little red does not frighten me. I am going to shoot now unless you do as *I* say. This is a sniper rifle. The bullets leave the barrel at high velocity. I am going to shoot my friend in the chest, through one of his lungs, and that same bullet will probably go into one of your lungs. You will have trouble holding on to my friend with a hole in such a vital spot. True, you will start to heal immediately, but before you do, I will put another bullet in my friend, and in you. How many bullets do you think you can take before you have to let go? How many bullets can you take before you die?" I pause. "I don't make many mistakes, Eddie."

My audacity shakes him. It shakes Ray as well; he turns a bit green. He continues to choke. Eddie reconsiders. "You will not shoot your friend," he says.

"Why not? You're about to kill him anyway." I settle on a spot on Ray's belly, just below the rib cage. They are roughly the same height; the wounds should be identical, less serious than holes in the lungs. "I am going to count to three. One—two—"

"Wait," Eddie says quickly. "I'll make you a counter proposal."

I keep my aim fast. "Yes?"

"I will tell you where your other friend is—as a sign of good faith—and you will allow me to leave with your boyfriend as far as the other end of the warehouse. There I will release him."

He's lying. He will break Ray's neck as soon as he puts some distance between us. "First tell me where Yaksha is, then I will consider your proposal."

Eddie snorts. "You are one cunning bitch."

"Thank you. Where is Yaksha?"

"He's not far."

"I tire of this." I put four pounds on a five-pound trigger. "Ray," I say gently, "after I shoot, I want you to fight to shake free. He will try to hold on to you, of course, but remember he will be bleeding as badly as you are. And even though he is stronger than both of us, he is alone. Even if I have to put two or three bullets in you, I promise, you will not die." My tone becomes bitter. "But you, Eddie, will die screaming. Like those people you tortured last night."

He is a cruel devil. "I look forward to hearing *your* screams."

I fire. The bullet hits where I intend and penetrates both of them, exiting Eddie's back and striking the passenger door of the gasoline truck. Red blossoms on Ray's midsection and he gasps in pain. But Eddie does not try to defend himself by continuing to use Ray as a shield. The guy is totally unpredictable. Instead, he throws Ray at me, momentarily knocking me off balance. Then he is on me. Yes, even though I hold the rifle in my hands and there are thirty feet between us, Eddie is able to get to me before I can get off another shot. He is like black lightning. Crashing into me with tremendous force, he knocks me onto my back. The rear of my skull smacks the ground and my grip on the rifle falters, although I have not let go of it. For a moment I see stars, and they are not Krishna blue but hellish red and threatening to explode. Stunned himself, Eddie slowly climbs to his knees beside me. He regains his concentration swiftly, however. His eyes focus on the rifle, the only thing that gives me an advantage over him. I try to bring it up, to put a bullet in his face, but once again he is too fast. Lashing out in a sharp karatelike motion with his right hand, he actually *bends* the barrel of the rifle, rendering it useless. He is bleeding badly from his stomach, but he grins as he stares at my broken toy. He thinks he has me now.

"I can take a lot before I die," he says, answering my previous question.

"Really?" I kick him in the belly, in his wound, and he momentarily doubles up. But my blow is not decisive. Before I can fully climb to my knees, he strikes with his left fist, and I feel as if my head almost leaves its place on top of my shoulders. Again, I topple backward, blood pouring from my mouth. I land dizzily in a pile of gravel. Pain throbs through my entire body from my face. He has broken my jaw, several of my teeth, at least. And he is not done. Out the side of a drooping eye, I see him climb to his feet and ready his sharp black boots to kick me to death. Out the other eye I see Ray also stand. Eddie has momentarily forgotten my lover, probably considering him small game.

Uncertain, Ray makes a move to attack Eddie that will lengthen my life by all of five seconds. Shaking my head minutely, I raise my bleeding arm in the direction of the truck. A look passes between us. Ray understands. Light the fuse, I am saying, detonate our bomb. Save the human race. Save yourself. I will keep Eddie busy for ten seconds. Ray turns in the direction of the truck, the gasoline from the other tanker puddling around the wheels. Of course Eddie also sees him turn for the truck. He moves to stop him. In that moment, summoning the last of my strength, I launch myself off the ground at Eddie's midsection.

We crash and fall into another painful pile. As we once more struggle to stand, he reaches over and grabs me by the hair, pulling my face close to his. His breath is foul; I believe he not only sucks his victims dry, but eats them as well. He looks as if he would like to take a bite out of me. His eyes are crazed: excited and furious at the same time. Prozac would not help him. He yanks at my hair and a thousand roots come out.

"That hurts," I say.

He grins, cocking his fist back. "Try this on for size, Sita."

I close my eyes and wait for the blow. This one, I am sure, will send me into the promised land. I just hope I have bought Ray enough time. What I do not understand is that Ray is still trying to buy me time. The blow never arrives. Ray's voice comes to me as if from far away.

"Eddie," he says firmly.

I open my eyes. Eddie and I both look over and discover that rather than follow my last instruction and light the fuse, Ray has chosen to punch a hole in the tanker with his fist. The gasoline pours out beside him like a gusher from a cracking dam. Of greater note, he has already struck a single wooden match and holds the flame above his head like a miniature torch that will lead us safely past the valley of the shadow of death. Or else straight into it. I am fully aware that the fumes of gasoline are more volatile than the actual liquid itself. And Ray stands in a cloud of petroleum fog. Not that Eddie and I loiter at a safe distance. Gasoline soaks both sets of our feet.

"I only have one match," Ray says to Eddie. "If you do not let Sita go, I will have to drop this one. What do you say?"

Eddie just won't learn. "You're bluffing," he says.

I catch Ray's eye. "No," I plead.

Ray smiles faintly in my direction. "Run, Sita. Fly. Return and fight him another day. In the end you'll win. Remember, you have Krishna's grace." His fingers move.

"Ray!" I scream.

He lets go of the burning match. Eddie lets go of me, in a hurry. For a moment I stare transfixed as the little orange flame topples toward the waterfall of gasoline. Despite my endless years, the countless deaths I have witnessed, it strikes me as inconceivable that such a tiny flame has the potential to scorch my universe, to burn everything I love and cherish. Yet my state of denial does not last forever. The match is halfway to the ground when I bolt toward Ray. But even I, Yaksha's prime pupil, am too slow for gravity. Before I can reach Ray's hands, which he holds up to ward me off, the match kisses the flowing river of fuel.

"No!" I cry.

Combustion is immediate. The gasoline at his feet ignites. The flames race up his soaked clothes. In an instant my beautiful boy is transformed into a living torch. For a moment I see his eyes through the flames. Perhaps it is a trick of the light, but his brown eyes suddenly appear blue to me, shining with the light of stars I have never seen, or stars I no longer remember. There is no pain on his face; he has made his choice willingly, to save me, to save us all. He stands for a moment like a candle fit to be offered to the Lord. But the flames are not idle; they rush toward me while at the same time they leap toward the truck that stands behind Ray. The truck is closer. Before my own legs begin to burn, before I can reach Ray and pull him free of the holocaust, the fire snakes into the opening Ray had punched in the tanker. The stream of fire is not a fuse we planned, but it is an effective one nevertheless.

The gasoline truck explodes.

An angry red hand slaps the entire front of my body. I have a last glimpse of Ray's fiery form disintegrating under the hammer of the shock wave. Then I am flying through the air, shooting through the smoke. A blur of a wall appears and I hit it hard and feel every bone in my body break. I slump to the ground, falling into a well of despair. My clothes are on fire, but they fail to light this black well because it is bottomless.

My last conscious awareness is of a sport coat being thrown over me.

Then I am blackness.

10 ~≈

I stand on a vast grass field of many gently sloping hills. It is night, yet the sky is bright. There is no sun, but a hundred blazing blue stars, each shimmering in a long river of nebulous cloud. The air is warm, pleasant, fragrant with the perfume of a thousand invisible flowers. In the distance a stream of people walk toward a large vessel of some type, nestled between the hills. The ship is violet, glowing; the bright rays that stab forth from it seem to reach to the stars. Somehow I know that it is about to leave and that I am supposed to be on it. Yet, before I depart, there is something I have to discuss with Lord Krishna.

He stands beside me on the wide plain, his gold flute in his right hand, a red lotus flower in his left. His dress is simple, as is mine—long blue gowns that reach to the ground. Only he wears a single jewel around his neck—the brilliant Kaustubha gem, in which the destiny of every soul can be seen. He does not look at me but toward the vast ship, and the stars beyond. He seems to be waiting for me to speak, but for some reason I cannot remember what he said last. I only know that I am a special case. Because I do not know what to ask, I say what is most on my mind.

"When will I see you again, my Lord?"

He gestures to the vast plain, the thousands of people leaving. "The earth is a place of time and dimension. Moments here can seem like an eternity there. It all depends on your heart. When you remember me, I am there in the blink of an eye."

"Even on earth?"

He nods. "Especially there. It is a unique place. Even the gods pray to take birth there."

"Why is that, my Lord?"

He smiles faintly. His smile is bewitching. It has been said, I know, that the smile of the Lord has bewildered the minds of the angels. It has bewildered mine.

"One question always leads to another question. Some things are better to wonder about." He turns toward me finally, his long black hair blowing in the soft night breeze. The stars reflect in his black pupils; the whole universe is there. The love that flows from him is the sweetest ambrosia in all the heavens. Yet it breaks my heart to feel because I know it will soon be gone. "It is all *maya,*" he says. "Illusion."

"Will I get lost in this illusion, my Lord?"

"Of course. It is to be expected. You will be lost for a long time."

"I will forget you?"

"Yes."

I feel tears on my face. "Why does it have to be that way?"

He considers. "There was this great god who was master of a vast ocean. This ocean—you may not know its name, but it is very near to here. This god had three wives. You know how hard it is to please one wife? You can imagine how difficult it was to keep all three happy. Not long after he married the three, two of them came to him and asked for gifts. The first one said, 'O great Lord. We are the finest of your wives, the most beautiful. Reward us with special presents and we will be most pleased.' And the second one said, 'We have served you faithfully and love none other than you. Give us treasures and we will stay with you for the rest of your life.' The god laughed at their requests, but because he was pleased with them, he fulfilled their wishes. To the first he gave all the jewels in his ocean: the diamonds, the emeralds, the sapphires. To the second he gave all the colored coral, all the beautiful seashells. The third wife, of course, asked for nothing in particular. So he gave her the salt."

"The salt, my Lord? Is that all?"

"Yes. Because she asked nothing from him, he gave her the salt, which she spread out in the ocean. All the bright jewels became invisible, and all the pretty seashells were covered over. And the first two wives were unable to find their treasure and so were left with nothing. So you see the salt was the greatest of the gifts, or at least the most powerful." Krishna pauses. "You understand this story, Sita?"

I hesitate. There are always many meanings in his stories. "Yes. This nearby ocean is the creation we are about to enter. The salt is the *maya*, the illusion, that covers its treasures."

Krishna nods. "Yes. But understand that these treasures are not evil, and the goddesses who own them are not simply vain. Dive deep into this ocean and they will cause currents to stir that will lead you to things you cannot imagine." He pauses and then continues in a softer voice, once more looking at the sky. "I dreamed of the earth, and that is how it came to be. In my dream I saw you there." He reaches out and his hand touches my hair and I feel I will swoon. "You go there to learn things that only earth can teach. That is true but it is also false. All of truth is paradoxical. With me, there is never any coming or going. Do you understand?"

"No, my Lord."

He removes his hand. "It doesn't matter. You are like the earth, unique. But unlike the others you see before you, you will not come and go there many times. In your dream, and mine, you will go there and stay."

"For how long, my Lord?"

"You will be born at the beginning of one age. You will not leave until the next age comes."

My tears return. "And in all that time I am never to see you?"

"You will see me not long after you are changed. Then, it is possible, you may see me again before you leave the earth." Krishna smiles. "It is all up to you."

I do not understand what he means by changed, but have more pressing concerns. "But I don't want to go at all!"

He laughs so easily. "You say that now. You will not say that . . . later." His eyes hold mine for what seems a moment, but perhaps is much longer. In that brief span I see many faces, many stars. It is as if the whole universe spins below and completes an entire revolution. But I have not left the hilltop. I continue to stare into Krishna's eyes. Or are they really eyes and not windows into a portion of myself that I have striven so hard to reclaim? A tiny globe of light emerges from his eyes and floats into mine, a living world of many forms and shapes. He speaks to me in a whisper. "How do you feel now, Sita?"

I raise my hand to my head. "Dizzy. I feel somehow as if I have just lived . . ." I stop. "I feel as if I have already been to earth and been married and had a child! It is all so strange. I feel as if I have been something other than human. Is that possible?"

He nods. "You will be human for only a short time. And, yes, it has all happened already. You see, that is the *maya*. You think what you have to do, to accomplish, to perfect yourself to reach me. But there is no doer-ship. You are always with me, and I am always with you. Still, it is deep in your heart to be different from the rest, to try to do in one long life what it takes others thousands of lives to accomplish. So be it. You are an angel, but you wish to be like me. But I am both angel and demon, good and evil. Yet I am above all these things. Dive deep into the ocean, Sita, and you will find that the greatest treasures you find are the illusions you leave behind."

"I do not understand."

"It doesn't matter." He raises his flute to his lips. "Now I will play you a song made up of the seven notes of humanity. All the emotions you will feel as a human and as a vampire. Remember this song and you will remember me. Sing this song and I will be there."

"Wait! What is a vampire?"

But Krishna has already started to play. As I strive to listen a sudden wind comes up on the plain and the notes are drowned out. The dust rises and I am blinded, and I can't see Krishna anymore. I can't feel him near. The light of the stars fades and all goes dark. And my sorrow is great.

Yet I have to wonder if I have lost the song because I have become the song. If I have lost my Lord because I do indeed desire to be what I will become. A lover who hates, a saint who sins, and an angel who kills.

I awake to a world I don't want. There is no transition for me. I am in paradise, I am in hell.

"Hello?" a voice says.

Actually, I am in a cheap motel. Looking around, I see a chipped chest of drawers, a dusty mirror that reflects bare walls, a dumpy mattress. It is on this mattress that I lay, naked, covered with a sheet. In this reflection I also see Special Agent Joel Drake, who sits on a chair near the window and waits anxiously for me to respond to his query. But I say nothing at first.

Ray is dead. I know this, I feel this. Yet, at the same time I hurt too much to feel anything. I hear my heart pump inside my chest. It cannot belong to me, however. In my long life I have drunk the blood of thousands, but now I am an empty vessel. I shiver even though the room is warm.

"Yes?" I say finally.

"Sita." In the mirror I watch the reflection of Joel come and sit on the bed beside me. The soggy springs respond to the weight, and my body sags in the middle. "Are you all right?" he asks.

"Yes."

"You're in a motel. I took you here after the explosion at the warehouse. That was twelve hours ago. You have slept away the entire day."

"Yes."

He speaks without believing his own words. "I followed in your footsteps. I went to see the mother. She was in a strange state, incoherent, like a broken record. She kept repeating the location of the warehouse that blew up. She said little else."

"Yes." Clearly I pushed the mother's brain too hard, etched my suggestion in her psyche, set up an echo. I have done this in the past, and the effect is seldom permanent. The woman will probably be all right in a day or two. Not that I care.

"I immediately drove to the warehouse," Joel continues. "When I got there you and your partner were confronting that guy. I was running over just as the explosion happened." He pauses. "You were thrown free, but I was sure you were dead. You hit a brick wall with incredible force, and your clothes were all on fire. I covered you with my coat and put out the flames. Then I saw that you were still breathing. I loaded you in my car and was taking you to the hospital when I noticed . . . I saw with my own eyes." He has trouble speaking. "You started to heal, right there in front of me. The cuts on your face closed, and your back—it had to be broken in a hundred places—just knit back together. I thought to myself, This is impossible. I can't take her to a hospital. They'll want to lock her away for the next ten years for observation." He stops. "So I brought you here. Are you following this?"

"Yes."

He is getting desperate. "Tell me what's happening here. Who are you?"

I continue to stare in the mirror. I don't want to ask the questions. Simply to ask is to be weak, and I am always strong. It is not as though I have any hope. Yet I ask anyway.

"The young man near the truck . . ." I begin.

"Your partner? The guy who was on fire?"

"Yes." I swallow. My throat is dry. "Was he thrown free?"

Joel softens. "No."

"Are you sure?"

"Yes."

"But is he dead?"

Joel understands what I am saying. My partner was like me, not normal. Even severely injured, he could have healed. But Joel shakes his head, and I know Ray was blown to pieces.

"He's dead," Joel says.

"I understand." I sit up and cough weakly. Joel brings me a glass of water. As I touch the rim of the glass to my lips, a drop of red stains the clear liquid. But the color does not come from my mouth or nose. It is a bloody tear. Seldom have I ever cried. This must be a special occasion.

Joel hesitates. "Was he your boyfriend?"

I nod.

"I'm sorry."

The words really do not help me. "Did both tankers, at both ends of the warehouse, blow?"

"Yes."

"Did you see anyone run out of the warehouse after the explosion?"

"No. That would have been impossible. It was an inferno. The police are still going through the mess, picking out the charred bodies. They've cordoned off the whole area." He pauses. "Did you set those tankers to blow?"

"Yes."

"Why?"

"To kill those inside. They were your killers. But I don't want to talk about that now. What about the other man? The one who was with my boyfriend and me? Did he get away?"

"I don't know where he went. He was just gone."

"Oh." That means he got away.

"Who was that man?" Joel asks.

"I'm sure you can guess."

"Edward Fender?"

I nod. "Eddie."

Joel sits back and stares at me. At this young woman whose body was crushed twelve hours ago, and who now appears completely well except for a few bloody tears. I note the dark sky through the cracked window, the glow of neon signaling the beginning of another long night. He wants me to tell him *why*. But I am asking myself the same question. Why did it take five thousand years to find someone to love again? Why was he then taken from me after only six weeks?

Why time and space, Krishna? You erect these walls around us and then close us in. Especially when those we love leave us. Then the walls are too high, and no matter how hard we jump, we cannot see beyond them. Then all we have are walls falling in on us.

I do not believe my dream. Life is not a song. Life is a curse, and no one's life has been longer than mine.

"How did you heal so fast?" Joel asks me.

"I told you, I am not normal."

He trembles. "Are you a human being?"

Wiping away my bloody tears, I chuckle bitterly.

What was that in my dream? That part about me wanting to be different? How ironic—and foolish. It was as if I were a child going to sleep at night and asking my mother if I could please have a horrible nightmare.

"Ordinarily I would say no," I reply. "But since I'm crying, and that's a thing humans often do, then maybe I should say yes." I stare down at my red-stained hands and feel his eyes on them as well. "What do you think?"

He takes my hands in his and studies them closer. He is still trying to convince himself that reality has not suddenly developed a pronounced rip.

"You're bleeding. You must still be injured."

I take my hand back and wave away his question. "I am this way. It is normal for me." I have to wipe my cheeks again. These tears—I cannot stop them. "Everywhere I go, everything I touch . . . there is blood."

"Sita?"

I sit up sharply. "Don't call me that! I am not her, do you understand? She died a long time ago. I am this thing you see before you! This . . . this bloody thing!" Not minding my nakedness, I stand and walk to the window, stepping over my burnt clothes, lying on the floor in a pile. He must have peeled them off me; the material is sticky with charred flesh. Pulling the curtain farther aside, I stare out a landscape that looks as foreign from the world of my dream as another galaxy. We cannot be far from the warehouse.

We are still in the ghetto, still on the enemy's turf. "I wonder what he's doing right now," I mutter.

Joel stands at my back. "While you rested, I went out and bought you some clothes." He gestures to a bag sitting on a chair in the corner. "I don't know if they will fit."

"Thank you." I go to the corner and put them on: blue jeans, a gray sweatshirt. They fit fine. There are no shoes, but I don't need them. I notice my knife sitting on the chair beneath the bag. However, the leather strap that I used to secure it to my leg is not there. I put it in my back pocket instead. It sticks out a few inches. Joel follows my moves with fear in his eyes.

"What are you going to do?" he asks.

"Find him. Kill him."

Joel takes a step toward me. "You have to talk to me."

I shake my head. "I cannot. I tried to talk to you on the pier, and you still followed me. I suspect you will try to follow me again. But I understand that. You're just trying to do your job. I'm just trying to do mine." I turn toward the door. "It will be over soon enough, one way or the other."

He stops me as I reach for the knob. Even after all he has seen of me. He is a brave man. I do not shake his hand from my arm. Instead, I stare into his eyes, but without the intention of manipulation, the desire to control. I stare at him so that he can stare at me. Without Ray, for the first time in a long time, I feel so lonely. So human. He sees my pain.

"What would you like me to call you?" he asks gently.

I make a face. Without the mirror I don't know if it is very pleasant. "You may call me Sita if you wish . . . Joel."

"I want to help you, Sita."

"You cannot help me. I've explained to you why, and now you've seen why." I add, "I don't want you to get killed."

He is anxious. It must mean he likes me, this bloody thing. "I don't want *you* to get killed. I may not have your special attributes, but I am an experienced law enforcement officer. We should go after him together."

"A gun won't stop him."

"I have more to offer than a gun."

I smile faintly and reach up to touch his cheek. Once again I think what a fine man he is. Consumed with doubts and questions, he still wants to do his duty. He still wants to be with me.

"I can make you forget," I say to him. "You saw how I affected the mother's mind. I can do that kind of thing. But I don't want to do it to you, even now. I want you just to get away from here, get away from me. And forget any of this ever happened." I take my hand back. "That is the most human thing I can tell you, Joel."

He finally lets go of my arm. "Will I see you again?" he asks.

I am sad. "I hope not. And I don't mean that cruelly. Goodbye."

"Goodbye."

I walk out the door and close it behind me. The night is not as warm as I like it, nor is it cold, as I hate. It is cool and dark, a fine time for a vampire to go hunting. Later, I tell myself, I will grieve for Ray. Now there is too much to do.

11 ~~~

On foot I return to the vicinity of the warehouse. But as Joel said, the entire area is cordoned off by numerous police officers. From several blocks away I study the remains of the warehouse with my acute vision, perhaps subconsciously searching for the remains of Ray. The investigative crew, however, is working the ruins. Whatever was lying around outside has already been picked up and deposited into plastic bags with white labels on them. With the many flashing red lights, the mounds of ash, and the ruined bodies, the scene depresses me. Still, I do not turn away from it. I am thinking.

"But what he did do was tie Heather up in his

*bedroom closet, standing up and wearing his high
school letter jacket—and nothing else—and force her
to suck on Popsicles all night."*

The night I met the newborn vampires, I heard an
ice-cream truck in the vicinity, its repetitive jingle
playing loudly. In the middle of December in the
middle of the night. Then, when I visited Mrs. Fender,
I learned she had a large freezer in her house. Finally,
after parking my tanker outside the warehouse, I saw
out of the corner of my eye an ice-cream truck. From
where I stand now, I cannot see that same spot to tell
if the truck is still there. But with the security in the
area I think that it might be there, and I believe that it
might be important.

What kind of thing did Eddie have about Popsicles?

What kind of fetish did he have about frozen
corpses?

Were the fetishes related?

If Eddie did get his hands on Yaksha's remains and
Yaksha was still alive, Eddie would have been forced
to keep Yaksha in a weakened state to control him.
There are two ways to do that—at least, only two that
I know of. One is to keep Yaksha impaled with a
number of sharp objects that his skin cannot heal
around. The other is more subtle and deals with the
nature of vampires themselves. Yaksha was the incarnation of a yakshini, a demonic serpent being. Snakes
are cold-blooded and do not like the cold. In the same
way vampires hate the cold, although we can withstand it. Yet ice thwarts us as much as the sun, slowing
down our mental processes, hampering our ability to re-

cover from serious wounds. Going by Eddie's obvious strength and knowledge of my identity, I hypothesize that he has indeed gotten a hold of Yaksha *alive* and is keeping him in an extremely weak state while he continues to drink his blood. I suspect Eddie keeps him impaled *and* half frozen.

But where?

At home with Mom?

Doubtful. Mom is crazy and Yaksha is a treasure too dangerous to leave lying around. Eddie would keep his blood supply close. He would even take it with him when he went out hunting at night.

I find a phone booth nearby and call Sally Diedrich. Before leaving the coroner's office, I had obtained her home and work number. I am not in the mood for idle gossip, so I come right to the point. Before going into the stiff business, did Eddie used to be an ice-cream man? As a matter of fact, yes, Sally replies. He and his mom owned a small ice-cream truck business in the Los Angeles area. That's all I wanted to know.

Next I call Pat McQueen, Ray's old girlfriend.

I don't know why I do it. She is not someone I can share my grief with, and besides, I do not believe such a thing should be shared. Yet, on this darkest of all nights, I feel an affinity with her. I stole her love and now fate has stolen mine. Maybe it is justice. Dialing the number, I wonder if I call to apologize or to antagonize her. I remind myself that she thinks Ray perished six weeks ago. My call will not be welcome. I may just open wounds that have already begun to close. Still, I do not hang up when she answers after a couple of rings.

"Hello?"

"Hello, Pat. This is Alisa. I'm sure you remember me?"

She gasps, then falls into a wary silence. She hates me, I know, and wants to hang up. But she is curious. "What do you want?" she asks.

"I don't know. I stand here asking myself the same question. I guess I just wanted to talk to someone who knew Ray well."

There is a long silence. "I thought you were dead."

"So did I."

An even longer pause. I know what she will ask. "He is, isn't he?"

I bow my head. "Yes. But his death was not just an accident. He died bravely, by his own choice, trying to protect what he believed in."

She begins to weep. "Did he believe in you?" she asks bitterly.

"Yes. I like to think so. He believed in you as well. His feelings for you went very deep. He did not leave you willingly. I forced him."

"Why? Why couldn't you just leave us alone?"

"I loved him."

"But you killed him! He would be alive now if you had never spoken to him!"

I sigh. "I know that. But I did not know what would happen. Had I known, I would have done things completely different. Please believe me, Pat, I did not want to hurt you or him. It just worked out that way."

She continues to cry. "You're a monster."

The pain in my chest is great. "Yes."

"I can't forget him. I can't forget this. I hate you."

"You can hate me. That's all right. But you don't need to forget him. You won't be able to anyway. Nor will I be able to. Pat, maybe I do know why I called you. I think it was to tell you that his death does not necessarily mean the end of him. You see, I think I met Ray long ago, in another place, another dimension. And that day at school when we all introduced ourselves, it was like magic. He was gone, but he came back. He can come back again, I think, or at least we can go to him, to the stars."

She begins to quiet. "I don't know what you're talking about."

I force a smile, for myself. "It doesn't matter. We both loved him and he's gone, and who knows if there is anything else? No one knows. Have a good night, Pat. Have sweet dreams. Dream about him. I know I will for a long time."

She hesitates. "Goodbye, Alisa."

Hanging up, I stare at the ground. It is closer than the sky, and at least I know it is real. Clouds hang overhead anyway, and there are no stars tonight. I call my old friend Seymour. He answers quickly, and I tell him everything that has happened. He listens without interrupting. That's what I like about him. In this world of gossip a good listener is rarer than a great orator. He is silent when I finish. He knows he cannot console me and he doesn't really try. I respect that as well. But he does acknowledge the loss.

"Too bad about Ray," he says.

"Yeah. Real bad."

"Are you all right?"

"Yes."

His voice is firm. "Good. You have to stop this bastard. I agree with you—Yaksha is probably in that ice-cream truck. All the signs point in that direction. Why didn't you wait until you checked it out before calling me?"

"Because if he is in there, and I get him away from Eddie and the cops, I won't be of a mind to make phone calls."

"Good. Get Yaksha. He'll heal quickly and then the two of you go after Eddie."

"I don't think it will be that easy."

Seymour pauses. "His legs won't grow back?"

"This might surprise you, but I don't have a lot of experience in such matters. But I doubt it."

"That's not good. You'll have to face Eddie alone."

"And I didn't do so well last time."

"You did well. You destroyed his partners. But you have to act fast or he will make more, and this time he will not allow them to gather in one place and be so easily wiped out."

"But I cannot beat him by force. I have proved that to myself already. He is just too fast, too strong. He's also smart. But you're smart, too. Just tell me what to do and I'll do it."

"I can only give you some hints. You have to place him in a situation where your advantages are magnified. He probably cannot see and hear as well as you. He is probably more sensitive to the sun."

"The sun didn't slow him down much."

"Well, he may be more sensitive to cold than you. I suspect that he is and doesn't know it. He certainly seems sensitive when it comes to his mother. He's what? Thirty years old? And he's a vampire and he's still living at home? The guy can't be that fearsome."

"I appreciate the humor. But give me something specific."

"Take her hostage. Threaten to kill her. He'll come a-running."

"I have thought of that."

"Then do it. But get Yaksha away from him first. I think it's Yaksha who can give you the secret of how to stop him."

"You read and write too many books. Do you really think there is a magical secret?"

"You are magic, Sita. You are full of secrets you don't even know. Krishna let you live for a reason. You have to find that reason, and this situation will resolve itself automatically."

His words move me. I had not told him of my dream. Still, my doubts and my pain are too heavy for words alone to wash away.

"Krishna is full of mischief," I say. "Sometimes, so the stories went, he did things for no reason at all. Just because he wanted to."

"Then you be mischievous. Trick Eddie. The football players at our school are all bigger and stronger than I am. But they're all a bunch of fools. I could whip their asses any day."

"If I survive this night, and tomorrow night, I will hold you to that proud boast. I might tell your football team exactly what you said about them."

"Fair enough." He softens. "Ray was enough. Don't die on me, Sita."

I am close to tears again. "I will call you the first chance I get."

"Promise?"

"Cross my heart and hope to die."

He groans but he is frightened for me. "Take care."

"Sure," I say.

Sneaking into the secured area is not difficult. I simply leap from one rooftop to the next when no one is looking. But getting out with an ice-cream truck in tow will not be so easy. There are police cars parked crossways at every exit. Nevertheless, that is the least of my worries. Moving silently a hundred feet above the ground, I see that the ice-cream truck is still in place. A palpable aura of pain surrounds it like a swarm of black insects above a body that has lain unburied. Dread weighs heavily on me as I leap from my high perch and land on the concrete sidewalk beside the truck. I feel as if I have just jumped into a black well filled with squirming snakes. No one stands in the immediate vicinity, but the odor of venom is thick in the air. Even before I pull aside the locked door to the refrigerated compartment, I know that Yaksha is inside and in poor condition.

I open the door.

"Yaksha?" I whisper.

There is movement at the back of the cold box.

A strange shape speaks.

"What flavor would you like, little girl?" Yaksha asks in a tired voice.

My reaction is a surprise to me. Probably because I feared him for so long, it is difficult for me even to approach him without hesitation—even while seeking him out as an ally. Yet, with his silly question, a wave of warmth sweeps over me. Still, I do not stare too hard at what he has become. I do not want to know, at least not yet.

"I will get you out of here," I say. "Give me ten minutes."

"You can take fifteen if you need, Sita."

I close the compartment door. Only police cars are allowed in and out of the area. Not even the press has gotten through the roadblocks, which is understandable. It is not every day twenty-plus bodies are incinerated in Los Angeles, although, on the other hand, it is not that unusual an occurrence in this part of town.

My course is clear. I will get myself a police car, maybe a navy blue police cap to cover my blond hair. I walk casually in the direction of the warehouse, when who do I run into but the two cops who stopped me outside the coliseum: Detective Doughnut and his young prodigy. They blink when they see me, and I have to refrain from laughing. A box of doughnuts is set out on the hood of their black-and-white unit, and they are casually sipping coffee from Styrofoam cups. We are still a block from where all the action is going on, relatively isolated from view. The situation appeals to my devilish nature.

"Fancy meeting you here," I say.

They scramble to set down their nourishment. "What are you doing here?" the older cop asks politely. "This is a restricted area."

I am bold. "You make this place sound like a nuclear submarine."

"We're serious," the young one says. "You'd best get out of here quick."

I move closer. "I will leave as soon as you give me your car keys."

They exchange a smile. The older one nods in my direction. "Haven't you seen the news? Don't you know what's happened here?"

"Yeah, I heard an atomic bomb went off." I stick out my hand. "But give me the keys, really. I'm in a big hurry."

The young one puts his hand on his nightstick. Like he would really need it with a ninety-eight-pound young woman who looks all of twenty. Of course, he would need a Bradley Tank to stop me. The guy has a phony prep school demeanor, and I peg him for a rich dropout who couldn't get into law school and so joined the force to annoy Daddy.

"We're running out of patience," Preppy says, acting the tough guy. "Leave immediately or we're hauling your tight ass in."

"My tight ass? What about the rest of me? That sounds like a sexist statement if I ever heard one." I move within two feet of Preppy and stare him in the eye, trying hard not to burn it out of its socket. "You know I have nothing against good cops, but I can't stand sexist pigs. They piss me off, and when I get pissed off there's no stopping me." I poke the guy in the chest, hard. "You apologize to me right now or I'm going to whip your ass."

To my surprise—I could pass, after all, for a high school senior—he pulls his gun on me. Backing off a pace as if shocked, I raise my arms over my head. The older cop takes a tentative step in our direction. He is more experienced; he knows it is always a bad idea to go looking for trouble where trouble does not exist. Yet he does not know that trouble is my middle name.

"Hey, Gary," he says. "Leave the girl alone. She's just flirting with you is all. Put away your gun."

Gary does not listen. "She's got a pretty dirty mouth for a flirt. How do we know she's not a prostitute? Yeah, that's right, maybe she is. Maybe we should haul her tight ass in on a charge of soliciting sexual favors for money."

"I haven't offered you any money," I say.

That angers Gary. He shakes his gun at my belly. "You get up against that wall and spread your legs."

"Gary," the old cop complains. "Stop it."

"Better stop now, Gary," I warn him. "I can tell you for sure you won't be able to finish it."

Gary grabs me by the arm and throws me against the wall. I let him. When I am upset, I like to hunt. Actually, when I feel any strong emotion, I like to hunt, to drink blood, to kill even. As Gary begins to frisk me, I debate whether to kill him. He is way over the line as he pats down my tight ass. He is not wearing a wedding band; he will not be missed much, except perhaps by his partner, who is soon headed for a heart attack anyway, with his diet of greasy doughnuts and black coffee. Yes, I think as Gary digs into my pockets and discovers my knife, his blood will taste good, and the world can do with one less creep. He holds the weapon up to his partner as if he has found the key to a treasure. In his mind it is that way. Now, because I am a certifiable criminal, he can do what he wants with me, as long as no one is videotaping the proceedings. No wonder the people in this neighborhood riot from time to time.

"Well, look at what we have here!" Gary exclaims. "Bill, when was the last time you saw a knife like this on a college coed?" He taps me on the shoulder with the flat of the blade. "Who gave this to you, honey? Your pimp?"

"Actually," I reply, "I took that knife off the body of a French nobleman who had the audacity to touch my ass without asking my permission." I slowly turn and catch his eye. "Like you."

Officer Bill reaches out and takes the knife away

from Officer Gary, who tries to stare me down. He would have more luck staring down an oncoming train. Carefully I allow a little heat to enter my gaze and watch with pleasure as Gary begins to perspire heavily. He still grips his gun but has trouble keeping it steady.

"You're under arrest," he mutters.

"What is the charge?"

He swallows. "Carrying a concealed weapon."

I ease up on Gary for a moment, glance at Bill. "Are you arresting me as well?"

He is doubtful. "What are you doing with this kind of knife?"

"I carry it for protection," I reply.

Bill looks at Gary. "Let her go. If I lived around here, I'd carry a knife, too."

"Are you forgetting that this is the same girl we ran into outside the coliseum?" Gary asks, annoyed. "She was there the night of the murders. Now she's here at the burned-out warehouse." With his free hand he takes out his handcuffs. "Stick out your hands, please."

I do so. "Since you said please."

After holstering his gun, Gary slaps on the cuffs. He grabs me by the arm again and pulls me toward the patrol car. "You have the right to remain silent. If you choose to give up that right, anything you say may be used as evidence against you. You have the right to the presence of an attorney, either retained or appointed—"

"Just a second," I interrupt as Gary starts to force my head into the rear seat.

"What is it?" Gary growls.

I turn my head in Bill's direction and catch his eye. "I want Bill to sit down and take a nap."

"Huh?" Gary says. But Bill does not say anything. Too many doughnuts have made him gullible. Already he is under my spell. I continue to bore into his eyes.

"I want Bill to sit down and go to sleep," I say. "Sleep and forget, Bill. You never met me. You don't know what happened to Gary. He just vanished tonight. It's not your fault."

Bill sits down, closes his eyes like a small boy who has just been tucked in by his mother, then goes to sleep. His snores startle his partner, who quickly takes out his gun again and points it at me. Poor Gary. I know I am no role model for the war against violence, but they should never have let this guy out of the academy with live ammunition.

"What have you done to him?" he demands.

I shrug. "What can I do? I'm handcuffed." To illustrate my helplessness, I hold my chained hands up before his eyes. Then, smiling wickedly, I snap them apart. Flexing my wrists, the remains of the metal bonds fall to the concrete, clattering like loose change falling from torn pockets. "You know what that French nobleman said before I slit his throat with his own knife?"

Gary takes a stunned step back. "Don't move. I'll shoot."

I step toward him. "He said, 'Don't come a step closer. I'll kill you.' Of course, he didn't have your advantage. He didn't have a gun. As a matter of fact, there were no guns in those days." I pause and my eyes must be so big to him. Bigger than moons that burn with primordial volcanoes. "Do you know what he said as my fingers went around his throat?"

Gary, trembling, cocks the hammer on his revolver. "You are evil," he whispers.

"Close." Lashing out with my left foot, I kick the gun out of his hand. Much to his dismay it goes skidding down the block. I continue in a sweet voice, "What he said was, 'You are a witch.' You see, they believed in witches in those days." Slowly, deliberately, I reach over and grab my pale white victim by the collar and pull him toward me. "Do you believe in witches, Gary?"

He is a mask of fear, a bodysuit of twitches. "No," he mumbles.

I grin and lick his throat. "Do you believe in vampires?"

Incredibly he starts to cry. "No."

"There, there," I say as I stroke his head. "You must believe in something scary or you wouldn't be so upset. Tell me, what kind of monster do you think I am?"

"Please let me go."

I shake my head sadly. "I'm afraid I can't do that, even though you did say please. Your fellow cops are just around the block. If I let you go, you'll run to them and tell them that I'm a prostitute who carries a concealed weapon. By the way, that wasn't a very flattering description. No one has ever paid me for sex, at least not with money." I choke him a little. "But they have paid me with their blood."

His tears are a river. "Oh, God."

I nod. "You go right ahead and pray to God. This might surprise you, but I met him once. He probably wouldn't approve of the torture I'm putting you through, but since he let me live, he must have known I would eventually meet you and kill you. Anyway, since he just killed my lover, I don't know if I care what he thinks." I scratch Gary with my thumbnail, and he begins to bleed. The red liquid sinks into his clean starched shirt collar like a line of angry graffiti. Leaning toward his neck, I open my mouth. "I am going to enjoy this," I mutter.

He clenches his eyes shut and cries, "I have a girlfriend!"

I pause. "Gary," I say patiently. "The line is 'I have a wife and two children.' Sometimes I listen to such pleas. Sometimes not. The French nobleman had ten kids, but since he had three wives at the same time, I was not inclined to be lenient." His blood smells good, especially after my hard day and night, but something holds me at bay. "How long have you known this girl?" I ask.

"Six months."

"Do you love her?"

"Yes."

"What's her name?"

He opens his eyes and peers at me. "Lori."

I smile. "Does she believe in vampires?"

"Lori believes in everything."

I have to laugh. "Then you must make such a pair! Listen, Gary, this is your lucky night. I am going to drink some of your blood, just until you pass out, but I promise you that I won't let you die. How does that sound?"

He doesn't exactly relax. I suppose he's had better offers in his days. "Are you really a vampire?" he asks.

"Yes. But you don't want to go telling your fellow cops that. You'll lose your job—and maybe your girlfriend, too. Just tell them some punk stole your car when you weren't watching. That's what I'm going to do as soon as you black out. Trust me, I need it." I squeeze him a little just to let him know I am still a strong little bitch. "Does this sound fair?"

He begins to see he has no choice in the matter. "Will it hurt?"

"Yes, but it will be a good hurt, Gary."

With that I open his veins farther and close my hungry lips over his flesh. I am, after all, in a terrible hurry. But only as I drink do I realize that his having a girlfriend has nothing to do with my letting him live. For the first time in my life the blood does not satisfy me. Just the feel of it in my mouth, the smell of it in my nostrils, revolts me. I do not kill him because I am tired of killing—finally. My prattle with the cops was a diversion for myself. The weight of knowing that I am the only one who can stop Eddie, the pain of my loss—they send sharp stakes into my heart that I cannot pull free. For once I cannot drown my trials in blood as I have drowned so many other difficult times over the centuries. I wish that I were not a vampire, but a normal human being who could take solace in the arms of someone who does not kill to live. My dream haunts me, my soul desire. The red tears return. I no longer want to be different.

Gary barely starts to moan in pleasure and pain when I release him. As he slumps to the ground, dazed, I reach over and grab his keys and cap and get in the patrol car. My plan is simple. I will put what is left of Yaksha in the car and then slip through the barricade with a tip of my cap and a hard stare at whoever is in charge of security. I will take Yaksha to a lonely spot. There we will talk, of magic perhaps. Of death, certainly.

12 ~~~

I drive to the sea, not far from where I killed the woman the previous night. On the way there Yaksha rests on the seat beside me, what is left of him—a ruined torso shrouded at the base in an oily canvas sack that protrudes with the steel stakes Eddie has driven into him to keep him in pain. We do not talk. As I loaded him into the patrol car, I tried to pull off this hideous sack and remove the spikes, but he stopped me. He did not want me to see what had become of him. His dark eyes, still beautiful despite everything that has happened, held mine. The words passed unspoken between us. *I want you to remember me the way I was.* And I prefer to.

The surf has quieted from the night before. The sea

is almost as calm as a lake, and I remember a time Yaksha took me to a huge lake in southern India only a month before we met Krishna. It was at night, naturally. He wanted to show me a treasure he'd found under the water. Yaksha had a special gift for locating precious jewels and gold. He was simply drawn to them: secret caves, buried mines—they grabbed him like a magnet. Yet, when he found these things, he never kept them. It was as if he just wanted to see what beauty the past had left behind for us to discover.

He told me, however, that this particular lake had a whole city beneath it, and that no one knew. He believed it was over a hundred thousand years old, the last remnant of a great civilization that history had forgotten. Taking me by the hand, he led me into the water. Then we were diving deep. In those days I could go for half an hour without having to take a breath. Yaksha, I think, could last for hours without air. Being vampires, we could see fairly well, even in the dark and murky water. We went down over a hundred feet, and then the city was upon us: pillared halls, marble paths, sculpted fountains, all inlaid with silver and gold, now flooded with so many drops of water that they would never again sparkle in the sun. The city awed me, that it could simply exist completely unknown, so beautiful, so timeless. It also saddened me, for the same reasons.

Yaksha led me into what must have been a temple. Tall stained-glass windows, many still sound, surrounded the vast interior, which rose step by step in concentric circles, a series of pews that climbed all the way up the wall to a stone ceiling. The temple was unique in that there were no paintings, no statues. I understood that this was a race that worshiped the formless God, and I had to wonder if that was why they went the way they did, into extinction. But as Yaksha floated beside me, there was a joy in his eyes I had never seen before. He came from the abyss, I thought, and maybe it was as if he had finally found his people. Not that they were demons like him, certainly, but they seemed to come from beyond the world. I, too, in that moment felt as if I belonged, and it made me wonder where I had come from. Yaksha must have sensed the thoughts in me because he nodded, as if we had accomplished our purpose in coming, and brought me back to the surface. I remember how bright the stars looked as we emerged from that lost city. For some reason, from then on, the stars always shone with a special luster when I was near a large body of water.

In the present moment the clouds have fled and the stars are bright as I lay him on his back not far from the water, although the light of nearby Los Angeles dims the definition of the Milky Way. How much modern civilization has lost, I think, when they lost the awareness of the billions of stars overhead. Unfortunately, my awareness is also rooted to the earth this night. Eddie has actually sewn the canvas bag covering Yaksha *into his flesh*. The unseen spikes twitch under the material, or maybe it is the dissected muscles that shake. A wave of nausea passes through me as I think of the torture he has endured. Reaching out, I touch my hand to his still cold forehead.

"Yaksha," I say.

His head rolls to one side. His lustrous dark eyes stare at the water with such longing. I know somehow that, like myself, he thinks of the lost city. That afternoon had been our last intimate moment together, before Krishna came on the scene and put a halt to the spread of the vampires by making Yaksha swear to destroy them all, if he wished to die with Krishna's grace.

"Sita," he says in a weak voice.

"There must be many hidden cities beneath the ocean."

"There are."

"You've seen them?"

"Yes. Under this ocean and the others."

"Where do you think all these people went?" I ask.

"They did not go to a place. Time is a larger dimension. Their time came, their time went. It is that way."

We allow some time to pass. The lapping of the small waves on the sand rhythmically echoes my breathing. For a minute they seem as one: each inhalation is a foam wave pushing up on the sand, each exhalation the pull of the receding tide. Over the last five thousand years the waves have reworked this coast, worn it down, carved out fresh bays. But even though my breath has moved in and out of my lungs all that time, I have not changed, not really. The ocean and the earth have known more peace than I have. They have been willing to change, while I have resisted it. My time went and I did not go with it. Yaksha is telling me that.

"That night," I say. "What happened?"

He sighs, so much feeling in the sound. "The moment you ran out the front door, I had the urge to walk to the window. I wanted to get a better view of the ocean. It reminds me of Krishna, you know, and I wanted it to be my last sight before I left this world. When the bomb went off, I was blown out of the house and into the woods, in two pieces. Landing, I felt myself burning, and I thought, surely I will die now." He stops.

"But you didn't die," I say.

"No. I slipped into a mysterious void. I felt as if I drifted forever on a black lagoon. The next ice age could have arrived. I felt bitter cold, like an iceberg drifting without purpose in a subterranean space. Finally, though, I became aware of my body again. Someone was shaking me, poking me. But I still couldn't see and I wasn't completely conscious. Sounds came to me out of a black sky. Some might have been my own thoughts, my own voice. But the others—they seemed so alien."

"It was Eddie asking you questions."

"Is that his name?"

"Yes."

"He never told me his name."

"He is not exactly a warm and fuzzy kind of guy."
Yaksha grimaces. "I know."

I touch him again. "Sorry."

He nods faintly. "I don't even know what I told him, but it must have been a lot. When I finally did regain full awareness and found myself in his ice-cream truck, I also found myself the captive of a madman who knew a great deal of my history, and consequently yours."

"Did he withdraw your blood and inject himself with it?"

"Yes. When I was in the morgue, he must have noticed what was left of me trying to heal. He has kept me alive so that he can keep getting more of my blood. He has taken so much, he must be very powerful."

"He is. I have tried twice to stop him and have failed. If I fail a third time he will kill me."

Yaksha hesitates, and I know what he is going to ask. His vow to Krishna, to destroy all the vampires, is in jeopardy.

"Has he made more vampires?" he asks.

"Yes. As far as I can tell he made twenty-one new ones. But I was able to destroy them all this morning." I pause. "I had help from my friend."

Yaksha studies my face. "Your friend was killed."

I nod. Another tear. Another red drop to pour into the ocean of time and space, which collects them, it seems, with no thought of how much it costs our supposedly immortal souls.

"He died to save me," I say.

"Your face has changed, Sita."

I look at the ocean, searching for its elusive peace. "It was a great loss for me."

"But we have both lost much over the centuries. This loss has but uncovered the change that was already there."

I nod weakly and put a hand over my heart. "The night of the explosion, I took a wooden stake through the heart. For some reason that wound never really healed. I am in constant pain. Sometimes it is not so bad. Other times I can hardly bear it." I look at him. "Why hasn't it healed?"

"You know. The wound was supposed to kill you. We were supposed to die together."

"What went wrong?"

"I stood and walked to the window. You probably beheld your beloved's face as you passed out and prayed to Krishna to give you more time to be with him."

"I did just that."

"Then he has given you that time. You have his grace. I suspect you always get what you want."

I shake my head bitterly. "What I wanted more than anything was for Ray to be by my side for the next five thousand years. But your precious God didn't even give me one year with him." I bow my head. "He just took him."

"He is your God as well, Sita."

I continue to shake my head. "I hate him."

"Mortals have always exaggerated the difference

between hate and love. Both come from the heart. You can never hate strongly unless you have loved strongly. The reverse is also true. But now you say your heart is broken. I don't know if it can be healed." He stops and takes my hand. "I told you this before. Our time has passed, Sita. We don't belong here anymore."

I wince and squeeze his hand. "I am beginning to believe you." I remember my dream. "Do you think if we do leave here that I will see Ray again?"

"You will see Krishna. He is in all beings. If you look for Ray there, you will find him."

I bite my lower lip, drink my own blood. It tastes better than the cop's. "I want to believe that," I whisper.

"Sita."

"Can you help me stop this monster?"

"No." His eyes glance over his ruined body. "My wounds are too deep. You will have to stop him alone."

His statement deflates what strength I have left. "I don't think I can."

"I have never heard you say you couldn't do something."

I have to chuckle. "That's because we've been out of touch for five thousand years." I quiet. "He has no weak spot. I don't know where to strike."

"He is not invincible."

I speak seriously. "He might very well be. At least in a fight with any creature walking this earth." I feel a sudden wave of longing for Ray, for love, for Krishna.

"I wish Krishna would return now. He could stop him easily enough. Do you think that's possible? That he will come again soon?"

"Yes. He may already be here and we don't know it. Certainly, when he returns, few will recognize him. It is always that way. Did you know I saw him again?"

"You did? Before he left the earth?"

"Yes."

"You never told me."

"I never saw you."

"Yes, I know, for five thousand years. When and where did you see him?"

"It was not long before he left the earth and Kali Yuga began. I was walking in the woods in northern India and he was just there. He was alone, sitting by a pool, washing his feet. He smiled as I approached and gestured for me to sit beside him. His whole demeanor was different from when we saw him the first time. His power was all about, of course, but at the same time he seemed much gentler, more an angel than a god. He was eating a mango and he offered me one. When he looked at me, I felt no need to explain how I had been doing everything in my power to keep my vow to him. We just sat in the sun and soaked our feet in the water and everything was fine. Everything was perfect. Our past battle was forgotten. I felt so happy right then I could have died. I wanted to die, to leave the earth with him. I asked him if I could, and he shook his head and told me this story. When he was finished, I didn't even know why he told it to me." Yaksha pauses. "Not until this night."

"What do you mean?" I ask.

"I believe he told me this story so that I could now tell it to you."

I am interested. "Tell me."

"Lord Krishna said that there was once this demon, Mahisha, who performed a great austerity to gain the favor of Lord Shiva, who as you know is really no different from Krishna. Because there can be only one God. Mahisha kept his mind fixed on Shiva and meditated on him and his six-syllable mantra—*Om Namah Shivaya*—for five thousand years. But Shiva did not appear before him, and so Mahisha thought to build a huge fire and offer everything he possessed to Shiva, believing this would surely bring him. Mahisha put his clothing and jewels and weapons—even his fifty wives—into the fire. And still Shiva did not come to him. Then Mahisha thought, what have I left to offer? I have renounced everything I own. But then he realized he still had his body, and he decided that he would put that in the fire as well, piece by little piece. First he cut off his toes, and then his ears, and then his nose. All these things he threw into the fire. Seeing this from his high mountaintop in the blessed realm of Kailasha, Shiva was horrified. He didn't want any devotee, even a demonic one such as Mahisha, cutting himself up like that. Just when the demon was about to carve out his heart, Shiva appeared before him.

"He said, 'You have performed a great and difficult austerity, Mahisha, and proved your devotion to me. Ask anything of me and I will grant it.'

"Then Mahisha smiled to himself because it was for

this very reason that he had undertaken his austerity. He said, 'O Lord Shiva, I ask for but two boons. That I should be unkillable and that whoever I should touch on the top of the head should in turn be killed.'

"As you can imagine, Shiva was not too happy with the request. He tried to talk Mahisha into something more benign: a nice palace, divine realization, or even a few nymphs from the heavens. But Mahisha would not be swayed, and Shiva was bound by his word, to grant anything asked of him. So in the end he said, 'So be it.' And then he quickly returned to Kailasha lest Mahisha tried to touch him on the head.

"As you can imagine Mahisha immediately started to cause all kinds of trouble. Gathering the hosts of demons together, he assaulted Indra, the king of paradise, and his realm. None of the gods could stop him because he was invincible, and, of course, every time they got near him, he would put his hand on the top of their heads and they would be killed. You understand that even a god can lose his divine form. In the end all the gods were driven from heaven and had to go into hiding to keep from being destroyed. Mahisha was crowned lord of paradise, and the whole cosmos was in disarray, with demons running wild, knocking down mountains, and raising up volcanoes."

"Were there people on the earth at this time?" I ask.

"I don't know. Krishna never said. I think there were. I think the ruins of the races I have found might have been from those times. Or maybe in the realms we speak of there is no time as we understand it. It doesn't matter. The situation was desperate and there was no relief in sight. But at the bequest of his wife, the beautiful Indrani, Indra performed a long austerity himself, with his mind fixed on Krishna and his twelve-syllable mantra—*Om Namo Bhagavate Vasudevaya.* Indra was hiding in a deep cave on earth at the time, and he had to meditate for five thousand years before Krishna finally appeared and offered him any boon he wished. Of course Krishna realized what was happening in heaven and on earth, but he did not intervene until after there had been great suffering."

"Why?" I ask.

"He is that way. There is no use in asking him why. I know, I have tried. It is like asking nature the same question about itself. Why is fire hot? Why do the eyes see and not hear? Why is there birth and death? These things just are the way they are. But since Krishna had offered Indra a boon, Indra was wise enough to jump at the opportunity. Indra asked Krishna to kill the unkillable Mahisha.

"It was an interesting problem for Krishna. As I have already said, in essence he is the same as Shiva, and he could not very well undo a boon he had freely granted. But Krishna is beyond all pairs of opposites, all paradoxes. What he did decide to do was appear before Mahisha as a beautiful goddess. The form he took was so ravishing that the demon immediately forgot about all the nymphs of the firmament and began to chase after her. But she—who was really a he, if the Lord can be said to have a particular sex—danced away from him, moving through the celestial forest, her hips swaying, waving her veils, dropping them along hidden paths so that Mahisha would not lose her, yet always staying out of arm's reach. Mahisha was beside himself with passion. And you know what happens when your mind becomes totally fixed on one person. You become like that person. Krishna told me that was how even the demons can become enlightened and realize him. They hate him so much they can't stop thinking about him."

I force a smile. "So it is all right if I hate him."

"Yes. The opposite of love is not hate. It is indifference. That is why so few people find God. They go to church and talk about him and that sort of thing. They may even go out and evangelize and try to win converts. But in their hearts, if they are honest with themselves, they are indifferent to him because they cannot see him. God is too abstract for people. God is a word without meaning. If Jesus came back today, nothing he said would make any sense to those who wait for him. They would be the first ones to kill him again."

"Did you ever meet Jesus?" I ask.

"No. Did you?"

"No. But I heard about him while he was still alive."

Yaksha draws in a difficult breath. "I don't even know if Jesus could heal me now."

"You would not ask him to even if he could."

"That is true. But let me continue with my story. In the form of the beautiful goddess, God was not too abstract for Mahisha. Because she danced, he in turn began to dance. He mimicked her movements exactly. He did so spontaneously, of his own free will, not imagining for a moment that he was in danger. He was fearless because he knew that he could not be killed. But the paradox of the boons granted to him was also the solution to the paradox. He had asked for two gifts, not one. But which one was stronger? The first one because it was asked for first? Or the second one because it was asked for second? Or was neither one stronger than the other? Maybe they could cancel each other out.

"As the goddess danced before Mahisha, in a subtle manner, at first almost too swift for the eye to see, she began to brush her hand close to the top of her head. She did this a number of times, slowing down a little bit on each occasion. Then, finally, she actually touched her head, and because Mahisha was so absorbed in her, he did likewise."

"And in that moment he was killed," I say, having enjoyed the story but not understood the purpose of it.

"Yes," Yaksha says. "The invincible demon was destroyed, and both heaven and earth were saved."

"I understand the moral of the story, but I do not understand the practicality of it. Krishna could not have given you this story to give to me. It does not help me. The only way I could bewitch Eddie would be to show him a snuff film. The guy is not interested in my body, unless it happened to assume the form of a corpse."

"That is not true. He is very interested in what is inside your body."

I nod. "He wants my blood."

"Of course. Next to mine, your blood is the most powerful substance on earth. He must have figured out that the two of us have grown in different ways over the centuries. He wants your unique abilities, and he can only absorb them by absorbing your blood into his system. For that reason I do not believe he will simply kill you outright when he sees you next."

"The first time we met he had a chance to kill me and didn't."

"Then you see the truth of what I say."

I speak with emotion, for all this talk does nothing to soothe my torment. Ray is dead and my old mentor is dying and God takes five thousand years to respond to a prayer. I feel as if *I* drift on the icy lagoon, hearing only gibberish whispered down to me from a black sky. I know Eddie will kill me the next time we meet. He will slowly peel off my flesh, and when I scream in pain, I know Krishna will not heed my pleas for help. How many times must Yaksha have cried out to Krishna to save him while Eddie pushed the steel spikes deeper into his torn body? I ask Yaksha this very question, but he is staring at the ocean again.

"Faith is a mysterious quality," he says. "On the surface it seems foolhardy—to trust so completely in something you don't know is true. But I think that trust, for most people, vanishes when death stands at the doorstep. Because death is bigger than human beliefs. It wipes them all away. If you study a dead Jew or a dead Christian or a dead Hindu or a dead Buddhist—they all look the same. They all smell the same, after a while. For that reason I think true faith is a gift. You cannot decide to have it. God gives it to you or he doesn't give it to you. When I was trapped in the truck these last few weeks, I didn't pray to Krishna to save me. I just prayed that he would give me faith in him. Then I realized it was all accomplished for me. I saw that I already had that faith."

"I don't understand," I say.

Yaksha looks at me once more. Reaching up, he touches my cheek where my red tear has left a tragic stain. Yet he smiles as he feels my blood, this creature who has just been put through such incredible pain. How can he smile? I wonder. There is a glow about him even in the midst of his ruin, and I realize that he is like the sea he loves so much, at peace with the waves that wash over him. Truly, we do become what we love, or what we hate. I wish that I still hated him and could therefore share a portion of his peace. With all I have lost, I fear to approach him with a feeling of love.

Yet I lie even to myself. I love him as much as I love

Krishna. He is still my demon, my lover, my enchanter. I bow my head before him and let him stroke my hair. His touch does not kill me but brings me a small measure of comfort.

"What I mean is," he says, "I knew you would come for me. I knew you would deliver me from my torment. And you see, you have. In the same way, even as he stuck his long needles into me and then injected himself in front of me and laughed and told me the world was now his, I knew that after you found me and heard Krishna's story, you would destroy him. You would save the world and fulfill my vow for me. I have that faith, Sita. God has given it to me. Please trust in it as I trust in you."

I am all emotion. I, the cold vampire. I shake before him like a lost little girl. I was young when I met him, so long ago, and in all that time I have failed to mature. At least in the way Krishna probably wanted me to. I know I am about to lose Yaksha, that he is going to ask me to kill him, and the thought devastates me.

"I do not know what the story means," I whisper. "Can't you tell me?"

"No. I don't know what it means, either."

I raise my head. "Then we're damned!"

Gently he takes a handful of my long hair. "Many in the past have called us that. But tonight you will make them repent those words because you will be their savior. Find him, Sita, bewitch him. I was every bit as powerful as he when I came for you that night I made you what you are. I did not come back willingly. You had bewitched me—yes, even then—and I was a monster every bit as corrupt as this Eddie."

I take his hand. "But I never really wanted to destroy you." He goes to speak and I quickly shake my head. "Don't say it, please."

"It must be done. You will need the strength of my blood. It is the least I can give you."

I hold his hand to my trembling mouth, but I am careful with his fingers, keeping them from my teeth. I do not want to bite them, even scratch them. How, then, can I drain him dry?

"No," I say.

His eyes wander back to the sea. "Yes, Sita. This way is the only way. And I am closer to it this time. I can see it." He closes his eyes. "I can remember him as if I saw him only yesterday. As if I see him now." He nods to himself. "It is not such a bad way to die."

I have had the same thought, and yet lived on. I do not deny him his last request, however. He has suffered greatly, and to make him go on as he is would be too cruel. Lowering my head and opening his veins, I press my lips to the flesh that brought my own flesh to this mysterious moment, which has sadly become a paradox of powers and weaknesses, of hopeless characters lost in time and space, where the stars turn overhead and shine down upon us like boons from the almighty Lord, or else curses from an indifferent universe. Yet the flavor of his blood adds color to my soul, and drinking it I feel an unlooked-for spark of hope, of faith. As he takes his last breath, I whisper in his ear that I will not do likewise until the enemy is dead.

It is a vow I make to Yaksha as well as to Krishna.

13

Once again I sit outside the house of the mother of Edward Fender. The time is eleven-thirty at night. Christmas is ten days away. Up and down the block cheap-colored lights, like so many out-of-season Easter eggs that have been soaked in Day-Glo paint, add false gaiety to a neighborhood that should have been on the late Soviet Union's first-strike priority list. Sitting in Gary and Bill's patrol car, I allow my senses to spread out, in and outside of the Fender home, around the block. My hearing is my greatest ally. Even the movements of worms through the soil a quarter of a mile away come to my sensitive ears. Mrs. Fender is still awake, sitting in her rocking chair and reading her magazines, watching a save-your-soul-before-

Armageddon Jesus program. She is definitely alone in the house, and I am pretty sure Eddie is not in the immediate neighborhood.

This puzzles me. With the police security near the warehouse and his confidence in the cleverness of his Yaksha hiding place, I can understand why Eddie left the ice-cream truck unguarded. But I cannot understand why he has left his mother wide open for me to take hostage. By now he must have figured out that I found the warehouse through her. Again, I am wary of a trap.

With Yaksha's blood in my system, my strength is back to a hundred percent, maybe even at a hundred and twenty percent, although I know I am still no match for Eddie, who drew upon Yaksha's blood many times over several weeks. Unfortunately, my state of mind is shaky. After Yaksha drew his last breath, I weighted the canvas bag that covered his lower portion with stones and waded out into the water and sank him. I made certain his remains are now safe from harm. He will never be found. Yet he has left me with a riddle I can't solve. Krishna told him his story five thousand years ago. Why was Yaksha so sure Krishna gave it to him to give to me for this particular emergency? For the life of me—and my life is very large—I can't see how I am going to destroy Eddie by dancing for him. For me, the word *faith* is as abstract as the word *God*. I trust that everything is going to work out for the best about as much as I trust that Santa Claus is going to bring me a bottle of blood for Christmas.

What can I do? I have no real plan except the obvious. Take Mrs. Fender hostage and force Eddie to come running, and then put a bullet in his brain when I get the chance. On my lap rests Officer Gary's revolver. Or is it Officer Bill's? It doesn't matter. It was in their car and it has six bullets in it. After tucking it in the front of my pants under my shirt, I get out of the car and walk toward the house.

I don't knock. Why bother? She will not open the door for me. Grabbing the knob, I break the lock and am on her before she can reach for the remote control on her TV. Modern Americans are so into their remotes. They treat them as if they were hand phasers or something, capable of leveling any obstacles. Fear and loathing distort her already twisted features. Yet the emotions are a sign that her brain has cleared. I am so happy for her, really. Grabbing her by the throat, I shove her up against the wall and breathe cold vampire air in her ugly face. Before burying Yaksha in the sea, I stripped down to nothing, but I was still wet when I put my clothes back on. The pants Joel bought for me drip on the wood floor as I tighten my grip on the old lady. Her weird gray eyes peer into mine, and as they do her expression changes. The bondage scares her but excites her as well. What a family.

"Where's your son?" I ask.

She coughs. "Who are you?"

"One of the good guys. Your son's one of the bad guys." I throttle her a bit. "Do you know where he is?"

She shakes her head minutely, turning a little blue. "No."

She is telling me the truth. "Have you seen him tonight?"

"No."

Another genuine reply. Odd. I allow a grim smile. "What did Eddie do as a kid for fun? Did he stick firecrackers in frogs' mouths and blow their heads off? Did he pour gasoline on cats and light them on fire? Did you buy him the gasoline? Did you buy him the cats? Really, I want to know what kind of mother it takes to make that kind of son."

She momentarily masters her fear and grins. The expression is like a crack in swamp mud, and smells just as foul.

"My Eddie is a good boy. He knows what to do with girls like you."

"Your boy has never met a girl like me before." I throw her back in her chair. "Sit there and keep your mouth shut." Taking the chair across from her, I sit down. "We are going to wait for Eddie."

"What are you going to do to him?"

I pull out my revolver. "Kill him."

She hardly blinks. In fact, on the whole she is remarkably accepting of my extraordinary strength. Her boy must have enlightened her on the new kids in town. Her fear continues to remain strong, but there is a cockiness to her as well. She nods as if to herself, her arthritic neck creaking like a termite-infested board.

"My boy is smarter than you. I think you'll be the one killed."

Turning off the TV with the remote, I cross my legs.

"If he's so smart, then why didn't he run away from home the day he learned to walk?"

She doesn't like that. "You're going to be sorry you said that."

I am already bored with her. "We shall see."

An hour later the phone rings. Since I hope to scare Eddie into rushing to the house, there is no point in having the mother answer and pretending that I am not here. Eddie will not fall for so simple a ruse anyway. I pick up the phone.

"Hello?" I say.

"Sita."

It is Joel and he is in serious trouble. In an instant I realize that after I left him, he went to this house, where he was abducted by Eddie. Eddie was here while I was rescuing Yaksha, probably outside hiding, probably confident I would return here the first chance I got. But when I didn't show, he took the man who rescued me from the flames, no doubt thinking he could use him as leverage with me. In a moment I understand that the chances of Joel living through the night are less than one in a hundred.

"He is nearby," I say.

Joel is scared but still in control. "Yes."

"He has made his point as far as you are concerned. Put him on the line."

"I am expendable," Joel says. "You understand that?"

"We're both expendable," I reply.

Eddie comes on the line a moment later. His voice

is liquid grease. He sounds confident, as well he should.

"Hello, Sita. How's my mother?"

"She's fine, busy boasting about her son."

"Have you hurt her?"

"Thinking about it. Have you hurt Joel?"

"Just broke his arms is all. Is he another boyfriend of yours? That last one of yours didn't last so long."

I strain to sound casual. "You win some, you lose some. When you're as old as I am, one is as good as another."

Eddie giggles. "I don't know about that. Right now I don't think you could do any better than me."

I want to antagonize him, make him act foolishly. "Are you making a pass at me, Eddie? Is that what this is all about? You want to rule the world so you can be sure to have a date for Friday night? You know, I talked to your old employer and heard what your idea of a good time is. I swear, with your social graces, I wouldn't be surprised if you're still a virgin."

He does not like that. It is good, I think, to find sensitive nerves before we again meet in battle. For all of Eddie's intelligence, he seems to have a fundamental immaturity when it comes to dealing with people, and I don't mean that he is simply psychotic. Many psychotics I have known have had excellent interpersonal skills—when they weren't murdering people. Eddie is a sorrier case. He was the nerd in the high school library at lunch picking at his zits and fantasizing about rape every time a cheerleader walked by. His tone turns mean and nasty.

"Let's cut to the chase," he says. "I want you to meet me at Santa Monica Pier in thirty minutes. If you are not there by then, I will begin to kill your friend. I will do so slowly just in case a flat tire has delayed your arrival. It's possible you still might be able to recognize him if you're less than twenty minutes late. My mother, of course, is to be left in her home unharmed." He pauses for effect. "Do you understand these instructions?"

I snort. "Oh, gimme a break. I don't jump when you say jump. You have nothing with which to threaten me. Such a thing does not exist on this planet. You want to talk to me, *you* get here within thirty minutes. If not, I will hang your mother's head on the front door in place of a Christmas wreath. The red color will be in keeping with the holiday spirit." I pause. "Do you understand my instructions, you foul-mouthed pervert?"

He is angry. "You're bluffing!"

"Eddie, you should know me better than that by now."

With that I hang up the phone. He will come, I am sure of it. But I have to wonder if I want him to bring Joel, if another standoff with an important life hanging in the balance will not cause me to falter again. Almost, I pray that he kills Joel before I am forced to kill him.

14 ～

A thousand years ago, in the Scottish Highlands, I was faced with a situation similar to the one that now confronts me. At the time I had a royal lover, the Thane of Welson, my Harold. We lived in a moderate-size castle on the northwestern coast of Scotland, where the biting winter winds blew off the foaming ocean water like ice daggers carved by frigid mermaids. They were enough to make me dream of Hawaiian vacations, even though Hawaii had yet to be discovered. I liked Harold. More than any other mortal I had met, he reminded me of Cleo, my old Greek friend. They had a similar sense of humor and they were both leches. I like horny men; I feel they are true to their inner natures.

Harold was not a doctor, however, like Cleo, but an artist, and a great one at that. He painted me in a number of poses, many times nude. One of these paintings now hangs in the Louvre in Paris, and is attributed to an artist who never even existed. Once I visited the museum and found a skilled art student painting a copy of the work. Coming up at his side, I just stood there for the longest time, and he kept glancing at me and getting more curious. Indeed, looking a little closer he even acted kind of scared. He wanted to say something to me but didn't know what. Before leaving I just smiled at him and nodded. Harold had caught my likeness perfectly.

At that time in Scotland there was an arrogant authority figure in the area, a certain Lord Tensley, who had a much bigger castle and ego than my Harold, but not the great object of his desire, which just happened to be me. Lord Tensley wanted me in the worst way and did everything in his power to woo me away from Harold. He sent me flowers and horses and carriages and jewels—the usual Middle Ages fluff. But I will take a sense of humor over power and money any day. Besides, Lord Tensley was cruel, and even though I have been known to bite a few necks in my day—and crush a few skulls—I have never thought of myself as one who enjoys pain at another's expense. One story had it that Lord Tensley had beheaded his first wife when she refused to smother their slightly handicapped female firstborn. All of Lord Tensley's subsequent lovers had stiff necks from checking their backs constantly.

While I was with Harold, I was going through one of my reckless periods. Usually I go to great lengths to keep my true identity secret, and it wasn't as if I romped around the Scottish Highlands biting the neck of every MacFarland and Scottie Boy who walked by in the dark. But during that time, perhaps because I was lazy and tired of arguing with people, I used the power of my eyes and voice to quickly get what I wanted. Naturally, after a time, I developed the reputation of being a witch. This did not bother Harold, as it had not bothered Cleo before him. Both were progressive thinkers. But unlike Cleo, Harold actually knew that I was a vampire, and that I often drank human blood. It really turned him on to have such a girlfriend. When he painted me, I often had blood on my face. Harold occasionally asked me to make him a vampire so that he wouldn't have to grow old and die, but he knew of Krishna and the vow I'd made to him and so he didn't press me. Once Harold painted a picture of Krishna for me from my description, and that was a work I treasured above all others, until it was destroyed in England in a German bombing raid during World War II.

Because I had shunned Lord Tensley, and had developed the reputation of being a witch, the good man of God felt it was his duty to have me tried and burned at the stake, a practice that was later to come into vogue during the Inquisition. In a sense Lord Tensley was a man ahead of his time. He dispatched a dozen armed men to bring me in, and because Harold's entire security force consisted of maids, butlers, and mule boys, I met the contingent myself before they reached our castle and sent their heads back to Lord Tensley with a note attached: *The answer is still no.* I thought that would scare him off, at least for a while, but Lord Tensley was more determined than I realized. A week later he kidnapped my Harold and sent a note to me stating that unless I surrendered myself promptly, he would be sending me Harold's head. Storming Lord Tensley's heavily fortified castle would have been a difficult proposition, even for a creature such as I, and besides, I thought a little feigned cooperation would bring Harold back to me all the sooner. I sent another note back: *The answer is yes, but you have to come get me. Bring Harold.*

Lord Tensley brought Harold and twenty of his best knights. Hearing them approach, I sent my people off. None were fighters and I didn't want them to get killed. Alone, I stood atop my castle gate that cold dark night with a bow and arrow in hand as the witch-squad rode up on their horses. The nervous exhalations of the men and animals shone like dragon's breath in the orange glow of the flickering torches. Lord Tensley carried Harold before him on his own horse, a jagged knife held tight at my lover's throat. He called up to me to surrender or he would kill my boyfriend before my eyes. The interesting thing about Lord Tensley was that he didn't underestimate me in the slightest. Naturally, one would expect the ten heads I sent back to him to make him cautious. But the way he maintained his distance, keeping Harold directly in front of him, and even the manner in which he avoided looking in my direction made me think he honestly believed I was a witch.

That was a problem. Generally in the past, before the advent of modern weapons, I could extricate myself from most situations by sheer speed and strength. An arrow or spear shot in my direction—I could just duck aside or catch it in midair. There was never a chance someone could defeat me in a sword fight, even when I didn't have a sword. It wasn't until guns were developed that I had to move more carefully and use my head first before my feet or hands.

For a long moment I licked the tip of the arrow in my hand and considered taking my best shot at Lord Tensley. The chances were excellent that I would be able to kill him without harming Harold. The problem was I would not be able to stop the other men from quickly chopping up my lover.

"I will surrender," I called down. "But first you must let him go."

Lord Tensley laughed. He was an intensely handsome man, but his face somehow reminded me of a fox that dreamed of being a wolf. What I mean is he was sly and proud at the same time, and didn't care if he got his snout bloody, as long as it was at mealtime. Harold, on the other hand, was as ugly as a man could be and still have all his basic features in the right places. He had broken his nose on three occasions, each time while drunk, and the sad thing was that each shattered cartilage actually improved his appearance. But he could make me laugh and he could make love all night and what did the rest of it matter? I would do my best to save him, I knew, even at the risk of my own life. Cowards I have always despised above all else.

"You surrender first," Lord Tensley called back. "And then we will let him go."

"I am all alone here," I said. "A frail woman. Why don't your knights come get me?"

"We will not debate with you, witch," Lord Tensley replied. And with that he stabbed his knife through Harold's upper right arm, a serious injury to receive in those days without modern surgical techniques and drugs. Even in the cold wind, I could smell the amount of blood pouring out of Harold. By bartering, I had made a mistake. I had to get to him soon.

"I will come down now," I called, setting aside my bow and arrow.

Yet I hung behind the castle gate even as I peered my head out at the wicked gang. Knowing they were coming, I had placed a fresh horse and supplies just beyond a nearby bluff. If Harold could get to the animal, I knew he would ride to a cave two miles distant that only the two of us knew about. There he could hide until his girlfriend extraordinaire figured out a way to wipe out the enemy. Harold had the utmost confidence in me. Even at that moment, bound and bleeding as he was, he smiled at me as if to say, give 'em hell. I was not worried about that part. It was keeping him alive at the same time that concerned me. But to that end I sought to focus my gaze on Lord Tensley as I looked out from behind the gate. He continued to avoid my eyes, however.

"Let him go," I called, pitching my voice as powerfully as I could, knowing, if given the chance, that eye contact would magnify my subtle influence tenfold.

"Come out now, witch, or I stab his other arm," Lord Tensley called back. "Then your heathen lover will be doing no more of those corrupt paintings of your filthy body."

Harold was in fact left-handed. I had to restrain myself from replying that if I was burned at the stake, then Harold wouldn't be doing any more paintings of me in either case. And as far as my filthy body was concerned—he hadn't minded the look and smell of it until I had told him to take a hike. Another phrase, by the way, that I think I invented. There is a place for sarcasm and this was not one of them. I stepped into the open and spoke steadily.

"Now you keep your word and release him," I said.

Lord Tensley did as requested, but it was a feint. I knew the moment he had me bound and gagged he would chase after Harold and either cut him down or recapture him to be tried as a witch alongside me. Still, Lord Tensley could not know about the horse I had waiting nearby, and for that reason I exchanged a long stare with Harold as they untied him and let him climb to the ground. Harold and I had a deep telepathic bond; it was another special element in our relationship. Even with the pain of his wound and the pressure of the situation, he was able to sense my mind. Common sense also came to his aid; he knew I would want him to get to the cave. He nodded slightly before turning and fleeing into the night. Sadly, he left behind a trail of blood that I could smell only too clearly.

When he was out of sight, I turned my attention to Lord Tensley's son, who had no reservations about looking at me. The young man was barely sixteen but large as an ox. He had one of those cheerful blank expressions that made me think that if his karma remained constant, then in his next life he would be a lineman for a professional football team and make two million dollars a year. Never mind that at that time there was no football, or even dollars for that matter. Some faces and things I just have a feeling for. It was my intention to send him on to his great destiny as quickly as possible, but I knew subtle suggestion would not work on his primitive brain. Stepping forward and focusing my eyes deep into his head, I said in a calm clear voice:

"Your father is the witch. Kill him while you still can."

The boy spun and shoved his sword into his father's gut. A look of immense surprise shone on Lord Tensley's face. He turned to me just before he fell off his horse. Of course I was smiling.

"I know you've kept one of Harold's paintings of me in your closet," I said. "I look pretty good for a witch, don't I?"

He tried to answer, but a glob of blood came out of his mouth instead of words. Toppling forward, Lord Tensley was dead before he hit the ground. Half the knights fled right then, including the athletic son, the other half stayed to fight. I dealt with them quickly, without mercy, largely because I was in a hurry to get to Harold.

But I was too late. I found him lying on his back beside the horse I had left for him. The wound in the arm had punctured an artery, and he had bled to death. My Harold—I was to miss him for a long time. To this day I have never returned to Scotland.

What was the moral of the story? It was painfully simple. One cannot argue with evil men. They are too unpredictable. Waiting for Eddie, with his mother firmly in hand, I know he will do something weird.

Still, I do not know what the moral of Krishna's story is.

15 ~

The smell of Eddie, even from four blocks away, is clear to me. Not that he makes any effort to sneak up on me. I assume this is because he values his mother's life as much as his own. His car stays at the speed limit. He parks out front. Two sets of feet come up the porch steps. Eddie actually pays me the courtesy of knocking. Standing on the far end of the living room with my gun to Mom's head, I call for them to come in.

The door opens.

Eddie has broken both of Joel's arms. They hang uselessly by the agent's side. Despite his intense pain, Joel strives to appear calm, and I admire him for it. He has many fine qualities—I really do care for the guy. Again, I have to tell myself that I cannot risk all of humanity for this one life. Joel flashes me a wan smile—almost in apology—as he is shoved through the door before Eddie. But he has no need to apologize to me, even though he has done exactly what I told him not to do. True courage, in the face of almost certain death, is the rarest quality on earth.

Eddie has found himself a gun, a 10-millimeter affair—standard FBI issue. He keeps it close to Joel's head and Joel's body close to his own. Eddie really does have a serious complexion problem. It looks as if when he was an adolescent he tried to treat his problem acne with razor blades. The experiment was a distinct failure. But it is his eyes that are the scariest. The green centers look like cheap emeralds that have been dipped in sulfuric acid and left out to dry in a radioactive dust storm. The whites are more red than white; his eyes are not merely bloodshot but hemorrhaging. Perhaps a local pollen irritates them. Maybe it's the sun I dragged him out into earlier. He looks happy enough to see me, though, and his mother. He flashes us both a toothy smile. Mom doesn't reply, not with my fingernails around her throat, but she does appear relieved to see her darling boy.

"Hi, Mom," Eddie says. "Hi, Sita." He kicks the door closed behind him.

"I'm glad you were able to make it on time," I say. "But I didn't mind waiting. It's been pleasant talking to your mother, getting to know what Edward Fender was like as a young man growing up in troubled times."

Eddie scowls. "You're a bitch, you know that? Here I try to be friendly in a difficult situation, and you try to insult me."

"I don't consider your trying to kill my boyfriend and myself an act of friendship," I say.

"You drew first blood," Eddie says.

"Only because I was quicker than your friends. Drop the B.S., Eddie, please. Neither of us is here to kiss and make up."

"Why are we here?" Eddie asks. "To play standoff again? That didn't work so well for you last time."

"I don't know. I destroyed your silly gang."

Eddie snickers. "You're not sure of that."

I smile. "Now I am sure. You see, I can tell when someone lies. It's one of those great gifts I possess that you don't. There is only you left, and we both know it."

"What of it? I can make more whenever I feel the need."

"Why do you feel the need? So that you can always have someone to order about? And while we're on the subject, what is your ultimate goal? To replace all of humanity with a race of vampires? If you study the situation logically, you'll see that it won't work. You cannot make everyone a hunter. There will be nothing left to hunt."

Eddie appears momentarily puzzled. He is intelligent but not wise. His vision is sharp but also myopic;

he does not look beyond next week. Then, just like that, he is angry again. His temper comes and goes like flares in a lava pit. Logic is not going to work on him.

"You're just trying to confuse me with that witchy voice of yours," he says. "I'm having a good time and that's all I care about."

I snort. "Well, at least now we understand your priorities."

He grows impatient. Pulling Joel tighter, he digs his thumbnail into Joel's neck, coming close to breaking the skin. "Let my mother go," he orders.

I act casual, even as I dig my nail into his mother's neck. "You have a problem here, Eddie. I hardly know this guy. You can kill him and I won't bat an eye. You're in no position to give me orders."

He tries to stare me down. There is power in his gaze but no control. "I don't believe you will just kill an innocent woman," he says.

"She bore you," I say. "She's not innocent."

In response Eddie pricks Joel's neck. The ice-cream man has a good feel for deep-rooted veins. The flow of blood is immediate and thick. Joel shifts uneasily but does not try to shake free, which he probably knows is impossible anyway. So far he has allowed me to play the game, probably hoping I have a card up my sleeve that I'm not showing. All I have is Krishna's abstract tale. But as Joel feels his life draining away, soaking his white shirt a tragic red, I understand his need to speak. Yet he has finally begun to grasp the stakes of this particular pot and is not afraid to die.

"He's not going to let me walk out of here alive, Sita," Joel says. "You know that. Take your best shot and be done with it."

The advice is sound. Using Mom as a shield, I can simply open fire. The only trouble is Joel is not Ray. He will not heal in a matter of minutes. He will certainly die, and still I won't be sure of killing Eddie. This problem—it is age old. To do what is right and save the day without destroying the very thing the day is lived for. I hesitate a moment, then dig my nail deep into Mom's neck. The woman lets out a terrified gasp. Warm blood spurts over my fingers. Which pump will run out sooner? I honestly don't know. Mom shakes visibly in my arms and Eddie's face darkens.

"What do you want?" he demands.

"Let Joel go," I say. "I will let your mother go. Then it will just be between the two of us, the way it should be."

"I will beat you to the draw," Eddie says.

I am grim. "Maybe."

"There is no maybe about it and you know it. You're not going to release my mother. You're not here to negotiate. You just want me dead."

"Well," I say.

"Just use your gun," Joel says with feeling. His blood drips off his shirt and onto his pants. Eddie has opened the jugular. I estimate Joel has three minutes to live. He will be conscious for only half that. Slumping slightly, he leans back into Eddie, who has no trouble supporting him. Although Joel struggles to remain calm, his color is white. It is not easy to watch yourself bleed to death. And what makes it worse is with his broken arms he can't even raise a hand to press over his wound. Naturally, Mom tries to stop the bleeding, scratching me in the process with her clawlike fingers, but I keep the red juice coming. They will both die about the same time, unless I do something quick, or Eddie does.

But I do not know what to do.

"Release him," I say.

"No," Eddie says. "Release my mother."

I do not reply. I begin to panic instead. I cannot stand by and watch Joel die. Yes, I, ancient Sita, the scourge of Krishna, who has killed thousands. But maybe my unchanging nature has finally been rattled. I am not who I was two days ago. Perhaps it is because of the loss of Ray and Yaksha, but the thought of another death on my hands chills me to the core. A wave of nausea sweeps over me, and I see a red that is not there, a deeper red than even the color of blood. A blotted sun sinking below the horizon at the end of the world. It will be the end of humanity, I know, to surrender to this maniac, but the mathematics of human life suddenly won't add up. I cannot spend one life to protect five billion. Not when that one life begins to wobble and sink before my eyes. Joel's blood now drips off the hem of his pants, onto the dusty floor. Mom's blood does likewise, through her frumpy nightgown. What is wrong with Eddie? Can't he see the seconds ticking by? His mother cries in my arms, and I actually feel sorry for her. Yeah, I know, I picked a wonderful time to turn into a softy.

"In less than a minute your mother will be beyond help," I explain. "But if you act now, I will heal her neck and let her go."

Eddie sneers. "You can't heal. You can only kill."

I harden my voice. "I can do both. I can show you. Just let him go. I will do the same with your mother. We can do it together, simultaneously."

Eddie shakes his head. "You're lying."

"Maybe, maybe not. But your mother is dying. That's a certainty." I pause. "Can't you see that?"

Eddie's cheek twitches, but his will doesn't. "No," he says.

Joel sags dangerously to one side and now has to be completely supported. There are two pints of blood on his shirt, two on the floor. His eyes are the color of baking soda. He tries to tell me to be strong and he can hardly get the words out.

"Just shoot," he begs.

God, do I want to. A bullet in the brain to put Joel out of his misery, then another five bullets in Eddie, in more choice spots than at the Coliseum. With his mother's life still in balance, I am confident I can get off all six shots without taking a bullet myself. But the balance is on the verge of tripping; the scale is about to break. Mom sags in my arms. There is no longer enough blood in her veins to keep her heart from skipping. She has strength left for her tears, however. Why do they affect me so? She is a terrible person. Krishna will not be waiting to welcome her on the other side, if there really is such a place. Yet, ironically, it is her very wretchedness that makes me pity her so. I don't know what's wrong with me.

I don't know what to do!

"Joel," I say, showing Eddie just how lousy my hand is by letting pain enter my voice. "I didn't want any of this."

"I know . . ." He tries to smile, fails. "You warned me."

"Eddie," I say.

He likes to hear the weakness in my voice. "Yes, Sita?"

"You are a fool."

"You are a bitch."

I sigh. "What do you want? Really? You can tell me that much at least."

He considers. "Just what I have coming to me."

"Christ." I want to throw up. "They'll kill you. This planet is only so big. There are only so many places to hide. The human race will hunt you down and kill you."

He is cocky. "Before they know what's happening, there won't be many of them left to do the hunting."

Joel's dripping blood is like a river, a torrential current I cannot free myself of no matter how hard I try. Once upon a time I enjoyed such red floods, but that was when I believed they flowed into an ocean. The endless sea of Krishna's grace. But where is he now? This great God who promised me his protection if I but obeyed his command? He is dead, drowned by the indifference of time and space like the rest of us.

"Krishna," I whisper to myself. "Krishna."

He does not appear before me in a vision and explain to me why I suddenly release my grip on Eddie's mother. The surrender is not an act of faith. The despair I feel in this moment crushes the breath of either possibility. The woman stands at death's door but somehow manages to stagger toward her son, with a twisted grin on her face that reminds me of a wind-up doll's. Her darling son, she believes, has conquered again. A sticky red trail follows her across the wood floor. Bereft of my mortal shield, I stand helpless, waiting for the shots that never come. Of course, time is on Eddie's side, and he probably has worse things planned for me. He waits while his mother comes to him.

"Butterfly," she says sweetly, raising her bloodless arms to embrace him. Shifting Joel into one arm, Eddie acts as if he is ready to hug her.

"Sunshine," Eddie replies.

Yet he grabs his mother with his free hand. Hard.

He yanks her head around. All the way.

The touch of the demon. Every bone in her neck breaks.

Hitting the floor dead, her eccentric grin is still plastered on her face.

Guess he wasn't that crazy about Mom, after all.

"She was always telling me what to do," Eddie explains.

The next minutes are a blur. I am told to surrender my gun, which I do. Joel is deposited on the couch, where he stares glassy eyed at the two of us, still alive, still aware of what is happening, but unable to do anything about it. Eddie does allow me to stop Joel's bleeding, however, with a drop of blood from my own finger. Eddie probably just wanted to see how it was done. On the whole, as Yaksha predicted, he is very interested in my blood. By remarkable coincidence he has a syringe and plastic tubing in his pocket—don't leave home without them. The modern medical devices no doubt facilitated his manufacture of other vampires. Pointing his gun at me, Eddie has me take a seat at the dining room table. He also has a tourniquet, which he instructs me to tie around my upper left arm. I am a role model of cooperation. My veins pop up beneath my soft white skin. It is odd that I should notice a mole on my elbow right then, one which I never knew I had, even though it must have been there for the last five thousand years.

I cannot believe that I am about to die.

Not taking his eyes or his aim off me, Eddie fetches a couple of glasses, and ice, from the kitchen. Clearly he wishes to celebrate his conquest with several toasts. I do not flinch as he sticks the needle in my largest vein and my blood traces a clear plastic loop into his glass. I'll have a Bloody Sita—on the rocks. The glass fills steadily. We look at each other across the dining room table. Joel is lying semiconscious ten feet off to my left, his breathing labored. From vast experience I know a large blood loss can cause a person to smother. In a few minutes I may even know it from personal experience. The grin on Eddie's face is most annoying.

"So I win," he says.

"What do you win? You're a miserable creature, and when I'm gone you'll still be miserable. Power, wealth, even immortality—they don't bring happiness. You will never know what the word means."

Eddie laughs. "You don't look so happy right now."

I nod. "That's true. But I don't fool myself that I am. I am what I am. You are just a caricature of a hero in one of your perverted fantasies. One morning, one night I should say, you'll wake up and look at yourself in the mirror and wish the person staring back at you weren't so ugly."

"You're just a lousy loser."

I shake my head. "I am not just talking about your ugly face. If you live long enough, you're going to eventually see what you are. It's inevitable. If I do fail to kill you tonight, I predict you will eventually kill yourself. Out of sheer loathing. One thing for sure, you're never going to change. You'll always be something sick that the creation just happened to vomit forth when God was looking the other way."

He snorts. "I don't believe in God."

I nod sadly. "I don't know if I do, either."

A wave of dizziness sweeps over me.

My blood, my immortal blood, is leaving me.

It will not be long now.

Yet I cannot stop thinking of Krishna, even when the tall glass is full and Eddie raises it to his lips and toasts my good health and drinks it down in one guttural swallow. It is as if my dream of Krishna and the story he gave to Yaksha have become superimposed over each other in my mind. Actually, it is as if I have two minds, one in this hell I can't block out, the other in a heaven I can't really remember. But the duality of consciousness does not comfort me. The memory of the bliss of my imagined conversation with Krishna on the enchanted hilltop just makes this bitter end that much more difficult to accept. Of course, I do not accept it. Even though I have surrendered, I have lived too long to lie down and be sucked dry like this. Krishna beat the demon by playing the enchantress. How may I play this same role? What is the key? If only he would appear before me now and tell me. Another glass fills and Eddie drinks it down.

"Now I will play you a song made up of the seven notes of humanity. All the emotions you will feel as a human and as a vampire. Remember this song and you will remember me. Sing this song and I will be there."

Why did he tell me that? Or did he tell me anything at all? Did I not just dream the whole thing? I had just lost Ray. My subconscious must have been starving for comfort. Surely I created the whole thing. Yet, if I did, the joy of the creation brought me more joy than anything in this world has. I cannot forget the beauty of Krishna's eyes—the blue stars wherein the whole of the creation shines. It is as if I trust in his beauty more than in his words. His love was a thing that never needed to be understood. The day we met, it was just there, like the endless sky.

The day we met.

What did he do that remarkable day?

He played his song on his flute. Yaksha had challenged him to a contest. Together they went into a large pit filled with cobras, and it was agreed that whoever came out alive would be the victor. Both carried flutes and played songs to enchant the serpents and keep them from striking. But in the end Krishna won because he knew the secret notes that moved the different emotions inside all of us who were present. With his song Krishna struck deep into Yaksha's heart and brought forth love, hate, and fear—in that order. And it was this last emotion that defeated Yaksha because a serpent only strikes when it senses fear. His body oozed venom by the time Krishna had Yaksha carried from the pit.

I have no flute on which to play that song.

Yet I remember it well. Yes.

"Sing this song and I will be there."

From that day, and that time outside of time, before there even were days, I remember it. My dream was more than a dream. It was a key.

Staring Eddie straight in the eye, I begin to whistle.

He pays me no heed, at first.

He drinks down a third glass of my blood.

My strength begins to fail. There is no time for love, even for hate. I sing the last song Krishna sang to us, the one of fear. The note, the tone, the pitch—they are engraved in my soul. My lips fold into the perfect lines of Krishna's flute. I do not see him, of course, and I doubt that I even feel his divine presence. Yet I feel something remarkable. My fear is great, it is true, and that emotion goes deep into my blood, which Eddie continues to drink. Anxiety crosses his face as he takes another sip, and for that I am glad. Yet beyond this I sense the true significance of my body, the instrument through which this song of life and death is continually playing for all of us. The realization even gives me a sense of the player, my true self, the *I* that existed before I stepped on this wicked stage and donned the costume of the vampire.

Again, I remember wanting to be different.

Eddie pauses with the bloody glass in his hand. He looks at me strangely. "What are you doing?" he asks.

I do not answer him with words. The tune continues to pour from my lips, a poisonous note with which I hope to save the world. The influence of it spreads throughout the room. Joel's breathing becomes painful—my song is killing him as well. It is irritating Eddie, that's for sure. He suddenly drops his glass and shakes his gun at me.

"Stop that!" he orders.

I know I have to stop, at least this melody. If I don't

he will shoot me and I will be dead. But another note comes to me, and it is odd because it is not one that Krishna played the day he dueled with Yaksha. Yet I know it, and once again I believe that the dream must have been a genuine vision. Before I entered the creation, Krishna gave me all the notes of life, all the keys to all the emotions a human being, and a monster, could experience.

I sing the note of the second center in the body—the sex center. Here, when the life energy flows, there are experienced two states of mind. Intense creativity when the energy goes up, intense lust when it goes down. Leaning toward Eddie, holding his eye as if it were his pleasure button, I pierce that secret note through his ears and into his nervous system and I send it *down*. Down even into the ground where I wish to bury his stinking body. It does not matter that I do not lust for him myself. It only matters that I have finally understood the meaning of Krishna's fable. *I am the enchantress.* The gun in Eddie's hand wavers and he stares at me in a new light. No longer does he just want my blood. He wants the container as well—my flesh. I pause long enough to give him a nasty grin. He resisted my suggestions before and my lover died. He will not resist me now and he will die.

I am that cheerleader he never had in high school.

"You have never had someone like me," I say softly.

Another note. Another inhuman caress.

Eddie licks his lips.

"You will never have someone like me," I whisper.

I do not sing the note. It sings itself.

Eddie fidgets, beside himself with passion.

"Never." I form the word with my wet lips.

One more note. I barely get it out.

Eddie drops his gun and grabs me. We kiss.

Hmm. Yuck.

I pull back slightly to let him adore the whole of me.

"I like it cold," I say.

Eddie understands. He is an ice-cream man, a connoisseur of frozen corpses. It is his thing and we should not judge him too harshly. Especially when he falls for my suggestion and drags me in the direction of the rear of the house. Toward the huge freezer where he used to go searching for Popsicles in the middle of the night. I am so weak—Eddie drags me by my hair. Yanking the fat white door open, he throws me inside, into the foggy frost, the cold dark, where his eyes are not as sharp as mine, and both our aversions to cold will stand or fall in critical balance. Landing on my ass, I quickly stand and find Eddie staring at me in that special way. I do believe he is not even going to give me a chance to fully undress. Tossing my head and hair to the side, I raise my right hand and place it on my left breast. One last time, just before I speak, I whistle the note.

"I do so prefer the dark," I say. "For me, it makes it that much more dirty."

Eddie—he has many buttons. This one makes his leg lash out. Behind him, the door shuts. The overhead light either doesn't work or doesn't exist. All is dark, all is cold.

I hear him coming toward me.

More than that I can distinguish a faint outline of him, even in the total absence of light. And I can tell by the lack of focus in his movements that he cannot see me at all. Also, already I can tell the cold has dulled his vampiric blood. This is both good and bad. The slower he is, the easier he will be to handle. Yet the same effect applies to me as well. My only advantage is that I know the dullness is coming. Unfortunately, snakes never mate on a winter night. The freezer puts a hold on his reckless passion just when I need it most. Before I can sing another note, he pauses in midstride, and I see that he realizes he has been tricked. In a flash he turns for the door.

I trip him. He falls to the floor.

In the event a large freezer door gets jammed and a person is locked inside, it is required by law that an ax be kept inside at all times. That way, if need be, the unfortunate individual can chop his way out. In Eddie's freezer the ax is strapped to the inside of the door, which is normal. As Eddie falls, I leap onto his back and over his head and grab that ax. It is a big sucker. Raising it over my head, feeling the weight of its sharp steel blade, I know true happiness.

"What's your favorite flavor, little boy?" I ask.

Eddie quickly goes up onto his knees, searching for me in the dark, feeling with his hands, knowing I'm near but not realizing what I have in my hands.

"Huh?" he says.

"Cherry red?" I shout.

I bring the ax down hard. Cut off his goddamn head. Black blood gushes out and I kick his amputated coconut into what could be a box of ice-cream sandwiches. Dropping the ax, I fumble in the dark with the door, barely getting it open. My strength is now finished. Even with the ax, even being a vampire, I would not have had the energy to chop my way out.

I find Joel dying on the couch. He has a minute more, maybe two. Kneeling before him, I lift up his sunken head. He opens his eyes and tries to smile at me.

"You stopped him?" he whispers.

"Yes. He is dead." I pause and glance at the needle still in my arm, the tourniquet and the plastic tubing. I twist the latter to keep it from leaking my blood onto the floor. Searching Joel's face, I feel such guilt. "Do you know what I am?" I ask.

The word comes hard. "Yes."

"Do you want to be like me?"

He closes his eyes. "No."

I grab him, shake him. "But you will die, Joel."

"Yes." His head falls on his chest. His breath is a thing of resignation, a settling of ripples on a mountain pond that prepares for a winter's frost. Yet he speaks once more, one sweet word that pierces my heart and makes me feel he is my responsibility: "Sita."

The seconds tick. They always do. The power of an entire sun cannot stop them even for a moment, and so death comes between the moments, like a thief of light in the dark. Eddie had brought a spare syringe. It sits on the dining room table like a needle that waits for me to poke in the eye of God. Krishna made me promise to make no other vampires, and in return he would grant me his grace, his protection. And even though I did make another when I changed Ray, Yaksha believed I still lived in that grace because I gave Ray my blood to save him, only because I loved him.

"Where there is love, there is my grace."

I believe I can save Joel. I feel it is my duty to do so.

But do I love him?

God help me, I don't know.

Stumbling into the dining room, I fetch the extra syringe. It fits snugly onto the end of the plastic tubing. Because I still wear the tourniquet, the pressure is on my veins and my blood will flow into his. Like Ray, six weeks ago, Joel will be forever altered. But staring down at his unconscious face, I wonder if any creature, mortal or immortal, has the right to make decisions that last forever. I only know I will miss him if he dies.

Sitting beside him, cradling him in my arms, I stick the needle in his vein. My blood—it goes into him. But where will it stop? As I sink into the couch and begin to pass out, I realize that he may hate me in the morning, which from now on will always come at night for him. He told me not to do it. He may even kill me for what I have done. Yet I am so weary, I don't know if I even care. Let him carry on the story, I think.

Let him be the last vampire.

TO BE CONTINUED . . .

MONSTER

CHRISTOPHER PIKE

Mary Carlson walks into a party with a loaded shotgun. In the blink of an eye she blows two people away – two friends. She wants to kill more, but Angela Warner, her best friend, stops her.

Now Mary's in prison and Angela thinks she is crazy. But is she? Angela investigates her friend's motive for the brutal murders – and discovers an unimaginable horror.

She should have let Mary go on killing.

Because now it's too late to stop the evil.

MASTER OF MURDER

CHRISTOPHER PIKE

Marvin is an eighteen-year-old senior in high school. He is also America's bestselling author of teenage fiction. In fact his latest series is the craze at his high school. But Marvin writes under a pen name and nobody knows who he is – and Marvin wants it to stay that way.

Now Marvin has a problem. The final instalment of his popular series is overdue, and he has no idea how the story should end.

But the problem gets worse. Somebody knows who he is.

Now Marvin is caught in a web of mystery more complex and frightening than his own books. And he realises that the story he has been spinning is true.

THE MIDNIGHT CLUB

CHRISTOPHER PIKE

Rotterham Home is a hospice for the young. It is a place of pain and sorrow, but also, remarkably, a place of humour and adventure.

At the hospice there is a group of five young men and women – the Midnight Club. Every night at midnight they meet and tell each other stories. Tales of intrigue and horror, of life and death. True stories, made-up stories – and stories which fall somewhere in between.

One night these five friends make a pact: the first one of them to die is to make every effort to contact the others – from beyond the grave.

Then one of them dies. And the story begins . . .

CHRISTOPHER PIKE

**Three of Christopher Pike's most popular books are
now out on audio.**

Look out for

**WITCH
BURY ME DEEP
FALL INTO DARKNESS**

BOOKS BY CHRISTOPHER PIKE

☐	50183 9	Last Act	£3.99
☐	49908 7	Spellbound	£3.99
☐	50590 7	Gimme A Kiss	£3.99
☐	53236 X	Remember Me	£3.99
☐	53037 5	Scavenger Hunt	£3.99
☐	54713 8	Fall Into Darkness	£3.99
☐	55679 X	See You Later	£3.99
☐	56889 5	Witch	£3.99
☐	58270 7	Master Of Murder	£3.99
☐	59020 3	Monster	£3.99
☐	59021 1	Road To Nowhere	£3.99

All Hodder Children's books are available at your local bookshop or newsagent, or can be ordered direct from the publisher. Just tick the titles you want and fill in the form below. Prices and availability subject to change without notice.

Hodder Children's Books, Cash Sales Department, Bookpoint, 39 Milton Park, Abingdon, OXON, OX14 4TD, UK. If you have a credit card you may order by telephone – 01235 831700.

Please enclose a cheque or postal order made payable to Bookpoint Ltd to the value of the cover price and allow the following for postage and packing:
UK & BFPO: £1.00 for the first book, 50p for the second book and 30p for each additional book ordered up to a maximum charge of £3.00.
OVERSEAS & EIRE: £2.00 for the first book, £1.00 for the second book and 50p for each additional book.

Name ....

Address ....

....

....

If you would prefer to pay by credit card, please complete:
Please debit my Visa / Access / Diner's Card / American Express (delete as applicable) card no:

Signature ....

Expiry Date ....

BOOKS BY CHRISTOPHER PIKE

☐	60698 3	The Eternal Enemy	£3.99
☐	58000 3	Die Softly	£3.99
☐	58268 5	Bury Me Deep	£3.99
☐	58269 3	Whisper Of Death	£3.99
☐	49909 5	Chain Letter	£3.99
☐	58001 1	Chain Letter 2	£3.99
☐	60697 5	The Immortal	£3.99
☐	61642 3	The Wicked Heart	£3.99
☐	61155 3	The Midnight Club	£3.99
☐	61158 8	The Last Vampire	£3.99
☐	61264 9	The Final Friends Trilogy	£3.99

All Hodder Children's books are available at your local bookshop or newsagent, or can be ordered direct from the publisher. Just tick the titles you want and fill in the form below. Prices and availability subject to change without notice.

Hodder Children's Books, Cash Sales Department, Bookpoint, 39 Milton Park, Abingdon, OXON, OX14 4TD, UK. If you have a credit card you may order by telephone – 01235 831700.

Please enclose a cheque or postal order made payable to Bookpoint Ltd to the value of the cover price and allow the following for postage and packing:
UK & BFPO: £1.00 for the first book, 50p for the second book and 30p for each additional book ordered up to a maximum charge of £3.00.
OVERSEAS & EIRE: £2.00 for the first book, £1.00 for the second book and 50p for each additional book.

Name...

Address..

....

....

If you would prefer to pay by credit card, please complete:
Please debit my Visa / Access / Diner's Card / American Express (delete as applicable) card no:

Signature...

Expiry Date..